The Seer

The Seer

G. Clifton Wisler

For the William Woods readers —
I hope you enjoy Scott's
adventures.

         G. Clifton Wisler

LODESTAR BOOKS
E. P. DUTTON · NEW YORK

Library of Congress Cataloging-in-Publication Data

Wisler, G. Clifton.
   The seer / G. Clifton Wisler—1st ed.
      p.   cm.
   Summary: Having recognized the fact that he is not of this Earth, fourteen-year-old Scott tries to live as a normal teenager while exploring his awesome powers of teleportation, matter conversion, and seeing the future. Sequel to "The Antrian Messenger."
   ISBN 0-525-67262-1
   [1. Extraterrestrial beings—Fiction.   2. Extrasensory perception—Fiction.   3. Science fiction.]   I. Title.   88-12896
PZ7.W78033Se   1988   CIP
[Fic]—dc19   AC

Published in the United States by
E. P. Dutton, a division of
Penguin Books USA Inc.

Editor: Rosemary Brosnan   Designer: Alfred Giuliani

Printed in the U.S.A.   W   First Edition
10 9 8 7 6 5 4 3

especially for Phillip

1

Scott leaned against the wall of the bus depot and looked out at the foreign street. The Kansas plain had been dull, flat, empty. Wichita, with its highway overpasses and streams of speeding cars and trucks, had at first seemed familiar. Now, staring at the half-deserted rows of benches all around him and at the empty sidewalk outside, he found no hint of the warmth and comfort of home.

Nothing's ever what you think it will be.

Hadn't Tiaf warned him of that? But Scott could only stand the lonely confines of his room so long. Then he'd get the urge to travel, to venture out into the larger world, and off he would go.

Bus depots were no good, though, he told himself. They were like wooden gates swinging in the autumn wind, allowing people to come and go at will. Depots, after all, were for people arriving and departing. Only a few, wanderers like himself, drifted through the waiting room with no place to go, nowhere to return to.

This could be a beginning, he thought. After all, no one knew him there. Wichita could be the setting for a great adventure, a wondrous exploration of sorts. But Scott also knew there was great peril. Being a stranger brought curiosity and suspicion, created misunderstanding and even fear.

He zipped up the front of his red windbreaker and slipped out the side door onto the street. A Dr. Pepper can rolled over against his toe, and he kicked it to the curb. A frowning policeman bent over and snatched it. Waving the can at Scott, the man dropped it into a nearby trash can.

"See there? That wasn't so hard, now was it?"

"No, sir," Scott said, shrinking back against the wall of the depot.

"I guess you didn't notice the sign, huh?" the officer asked.

Neatly stenciled across the trash can were the words KEEP WICHITA CLEAN TODAY FOR A BETTER TOMORROW.

"Sorry," Scott said, dropping his chin onto his chest.

"Well, so long as you remember," the policeman added. Scott nodded, then made a rapid escape down the street.

He walked aimlessly two or three blocks before arriving at a busier street. Shoppers filtered in and out of two large department stores across the way, and on the opposite corner of the intersection a dozen kids chased one another around a tall lamppost.

Suddenly Scott felt his head throb. The pain sent him stumbling, weak-kneed, back against the side of a newspaper rack. He closed his eyes and shook as a fiery light burned through his thoughts.

"Are you all right, little boy?" a grandmotherly woman asked as she touched Scott lightly on the shoulder.

Scott held his hands against his ears and pressed in hopes of keeping his head from exploding.

"Little boy?" the old woman asked.

Suddenly the pain subsided, and Scott gazed up into the woman's concerned eyes.

"I'm fine," he assured her. "And I'm fourteen!"

"Yes, I see that," she replied, helping him steady himself. "Can I help you to the café down the street? Maybe a cold drink would—"

"I'm fine," Scott barked. Then he sidestepped his way to the corner and hurried across the street.

Actually, though, he was far from fine. Bits of an image were surfacing in his head, and he couldn't sweep them away. He finally sat on the corner of a bus-stop bench and tried to blink away the vision. The wind blew against his face, burning his cheeks and sweeping strands of frayed blond hair away from his forehead. For a moment his blazing blue eyes scanned the street like a telescope, examining every inch of the place. He saw each shopper, studied the faces of mothers and daughters, sons and fathers, shopkeepers and bus drivers. He smiled at a small baby resting on its mother's shoulder. When he reached the tall neon sign bolted to the side of the Fremont Hotel, he froze.

3

The hairs on his neck rose, and an icy chill ran down Scott's spine. He closed his eyes a second. The image inside his head sharpened. The tall sign wavered as the prairie wind intensified. Then, amid sounds of splintering wood and grinding steel, the upper supports worked themselves loose. The sign fell, and . . .

Scott blinked the vision away. He opened his eyes wide and shook off a sense of impending doom.

No, he told himself. Not again! Tiaf warned against it. I have to get away from here!

But as he rose to his feet, the image of the falling sign pounded against his thoughts. And then he saw the children.

There were a dozen, maybe more, of them. The smallest, a blond-haired boy about ten years old, a boy who might have been Scott himself half a decade earlier, was battling to control a red knit cap. The older ones wrestled the cap away, though, then tossed it to and fro. The tormented boy hollered and pleaded and threatened, but the others only laughed and continued their game.

Scott covered his ears again, shutting out their laughter. But he couldn't silence the screams taking possession of his mind. The sign swayed, then fell. And from beneath its crashed beams and shattered neon tubes protruded a small hand . . . holding the red cap.

No! Scott silently screamed.

The vision was swept away by another. The stern face of Tiaf, Scott's guide and tutor, appeared, urging caution.

4

"There is a great danger in interfering with the natural course of events. History relies on random chance, and if you disturb the flow of events . . ."

Yes. Scott knew the risks.

"And what about the danger to yourself?" Tiaf's voice whispered. "You will become a curiosity, something to be put on display as at a museum or carnival. They will discover who you are, *what* you are. Better you should return to my side."

Scott gazed across the street. He envied the smiles on the faces of the boys and girls as they tossed the cap around their circle.

"Catch it, Ben!" they urged. Their little companion jumped higher and higher in his efforts to recapture the cap. The frown had left. It was now replaced by a playful smile.

You're lucky, Scott thought as he stepped to the curb and prepared to cross the street. That sign's going to fall, and you may all be killed, but just now I'd trade places with any of you. Because you're happy. And one minute of laughter is worth more than . . .

The WALK sign flashed on the far corner, and Scott hastened across. The policeman who had picked up the can was slowly making his way up the street, and Scott raced to his side.

"Well, been kicking any other cans?" the man asked with a smile.

"Sir, you've got to get those kids out of the way!" Scott cried, tugging on the officer's arm. "See them there? You've got to get them clear!"

"What?" the policeman asked, clamping his hands onto Scott's shoulders and freezing him in his tracks. "Slow down and tell me what you're talking about."

"It's that sign," Scott said, pointing to the tall neon sign still flashing FREMONT in large block letters.

"Oh?" the policeman asked, following Scott's eyes to the hotel. "What about it?"

"It's about to fall," Scott warned. "See the supports up there? The bolts are coming loose. The whole thing's about to give way, and—"

"Kid, you're crazy!" the policeman declared, giving Scott a shake as if that might clear the boy's head. "That thing's been up there since I was your age."

"I know what I saw!" Scott shouted.

"Saw?" the officer asked with widening eyes. "You just got into town on the bus, didn't you? Did you take something? What's your name?"

"Listen to me!" Scott shouted. "It's going to fall. You have to get those kids out of the way!"

People on the sidewalk began to back away. Some shook their heads and hurried down the street. Others mumbled to each other. A few laughed.

"Listen here," the policeman whispered, taking Scott aside. "Calm yourself. You're not from around here, are you? Maybe you ought to sit down a minute."

The vision throbbed inside Scott's head again, and he shuddered. Across the street little Ben managed to recapture the cap at last. He stood there, grinning and holding the cap in his hand as Scott's ears picked up the first sounds of popping bolts.

"Get away from there!" Scott howled, breaking loose

6

from the policeman and jumping out into the street. Horns blasted warnings, and cars screeched to a halt. "Hey!" Scott screamed at the youngsters. "That sign's going to fall! Get away!"

Most of the children raced away. Others were snatched by worried passersby. No one seemed concerned about the sign. All eyes were on the boy standing in the middle of the street, his arms waving at the sign like a maniac. A crowd began to gather. Two girls huddled beside the lamppost—beneath the very spot where the sign would fall.

No, Scott thought as he dashed toward them. A section of pipe lay beside the curb. Scott grabbed it and waved it at the children. Both cried out and fled toward safety.

"Now, steady yourself, son," the policeman said as he cautiously approached Scott. "There's no need of that."

"You don't understand!" Scott shouted. "It's going to fall. You have to get everybody away from here."

"What about you? Aren't you afraid you'll be hurt? You're standing right underneath it."

Scott shuddered as he glanced overhead. Were they all blind? Couldn't they see the supports were giving way even now?

"Well?" the policeman asked.

"Stay back!" Scott warned, waving the pipe.

Cars were already swinging wide of the corner. The gathering crowd blocked off traffic from the side streets. The throng began retreating when two other officers arrived.

"It's all right," the policeman said. "Put down the pipe, son. Come along with me. A good night's sleep and a square meal or two will make you feel a lot better."

Scott shrank back. Then the sign at last broke free of the first support. People screamed and darted away in panic. The policeman's eyes filled with disbelief as he turned and raced clear.

The pipe slipped from Scott's fingers as he backed up. His knees locked, and he fell to the sidewalk as plaster and brick began to rain down. The steel groaned, and sparks flew as the neon tubes shattered.

Scott took a large emerald ring from his pocket. For a moment he stared at the delicate letters stamped across the stone.

I told you, Scott silently said to the fleeing crowd. Then he closed his eyes and clutched the cold green gem. As steel and glass crashed downward all around him, his flesh grew numb. A chill took possession of his being. Then he was enveloped by a whirlwind of light and sound that swept him away.

2

Teleportation was a great mystery to Scott. He was unable to understand how concentrating on the sparkling center of an emerald could allow him to move from one place to another. And whenever he finally arrived, his mind always seemed scrambled. His senses were turned upside down. So it was that he wasn't altogether surprised to find himself stirring to life amid the confinement of metal bulkheads in a world totally devoured by darkness.

"Am I dead?" he asked as a swaying rhythm gently rocked his body.

No one answered, but the words echoing through the darkened chamber caused two panels of overhead lights to flicker and then brighten.

No, not dead, Scott realized as he recognized the familiar hard lines of his sleeping chamber. He was stiff and sore, though, as if someone or something had bat-

9

tered his body. And his eyes refused to come into focus.

Even so, Scott's ears were unimpaired, and he had no trouble detecting the subtle whisper of the compartment door opening. A tall, white-haired old man entered and sat down at the small, colorless table near the foot of the sleeping compartment.

"So, you've awakened," the old man said.

"Yes, Tiaf," Scott declared. "But I don't remember arriving. Always before, I—"

"It was a near thing this time, little friend," Tiaf broke in. "I found you outside, bruised about the head and shoulders and babbling something about a red cap."

Scott sat up and blinked the mist from his eyes. His chest and arms ached. When he unbuttoned his simple cotton tunic and bared his shoulders, he could see bruises on his chest and a wide cloth binding about his ribs.

"It must have been the bricks," Scott said, remembering. "It seemed like the whole world was crashing down on top of me. There was this sign, and—"

"I see it," Tiaf said, closing his eyes a moment. "It was dangerous, staying so long. Remember, we are messengers, we Antrians. Our gift is the seeing. If you must, tell what you have seen and leave. To stay is to imperil yourself."

Scott nodded. That was always easier for Tiaf, though. The old man had grown up in a world of telepaths and seers. Tiaf had been taught all the mysteries. He understood. For Scott, it was all new. He'd never heard of Antrians a year before. For fourteen years he'd thought himself the same as any other skinny, blond-haired, high school, Texas-city boy. Well, maybe he was a bit better at math, and he sometimes had premonitions. But anyone who would have suggested Scott was from another world would have been locked up in a private room with mattresses lining the walls!

"You are remembering," Tiaf whispered.

"Is that bad?" Scott asked.

"Bad? No, we all remember what's come to pass," the old man said sadly. "I, too, recall other times and places."

"Oh?"

"My home and friends, now all vaporized into dust out past the Orion Nebula."

"Not my mother and father. They came here, to Earth."

"So that you might be born. But there was the crash, and they, too, were gone."

"I never knew them, Tiaf. I miss my old family, Mom and Dad," Scott said as he touched the bandages on his sore ribs. "My brother, Brian, too. I know I was adopted, but I always felt like I belonged there."

"And not here?" Tiaf asked, rising slowly and stepping to the hard metallic shelf that served as a bed.

"No," Scott grumbled. "I know I can't go back. After all, they think I'm dead. I appreciate your teaching me things, but I miss being around other kids, sleeping on a real bed, going camping or fishing, and staring at the stars."

11

"You can do as you wish," Tiaf pointed out.

"For how long?" Scott asked. "A day? Two? I wasn't out two hours this time."

"Yes," Tiaf said, grinning as he produced a Wichita newspaper. A large headline read Mystery Boy Saves Children.

"I did it again, didn't I?"

Scott's head began to throb as he recalled the horrible scene, the bricks and glass raining down as he focused on the emerald. Tiaf drew out a small device and placed it alongside Scott's neck. A warm, pulsating hum worked its way through his being, and the pain passed in an instant.

"It's a shame you can't heal bruised ribs that easily," Scott complained. "I'd like to see you have the paramedics out to this place. One look at this ship, and they'd be the ones needing C.P.R.!"

"Healing is an art," Tiaf said, setting the vibrator aside for a moment and placing his fingers on Scott's forehead. "Your mind is capable of transforming matter, though. Just as you can move yourself from place to place, Scott, so you can rearrange molecules as you wish."

"You mean I can make the bruises go away?"

"I'll help you. Look at them, then think hard at how the flesh appeared before."

"And my ribs?"

"Think of them as whole."

"It's the same way we make people think the ship is an old barn or a cave, isn't it?"

"No," Tiaf said, shaking his head and drawing back

12

his hands. "That is easy. We shape the images in the minds of others. What you will do now is to change matter. Your ribs won't *appear* to be well. They *will be* well."

"What do you call that?" Scott asked.

"Matter conversion."

"You mean I can stare at a tree and change it into a car?"

"No," Tiaf said, smiling. "You can't change the molecular elements themselves. You could convert a tree into a wooden bench or a ladder."

"Or a bigger tree?"

"Yes, of a different height or shape. And if you concentrate on the ring, you can make things appear."

"You mean if I don't like how I look, I can just change things around so I'm different?"

"It's been done. We change clothing, for instance, when we travel dimensionally."

"You mean when you go back in time, you can change your tunic into a Roman toga? I like that. Kids could have a great time on Halloween doing that. Why buy a costume when you can change yourself into an ogre or a witch?"

Tiaf appeared confused, and Scott laughed. He often forgot Tiaf wasn't schooled in such traditions as Halloween.

"This matter conversion, is it something I can do now?" Scott asked.

"It's a learned skill," Tiaf explained. "You have great talents, though. You will acquire it swiftly, I suspect."

"Then let's get started," Scott said enthusiastically. "These ribs hurt."

Tiaf grinned, then placed his fingers to Scott's temples.

"Close your eyes and imagine the flesh mended," Tiaf instructed. Scott did just that. At first nothing happened. Then Scott felt a warm glow. The ache began to fade, and in half an hour, even the bruises had vanished.

"That's better," Scott said as Tiaf cut away the bindings from his ribs. "I could've been flat on my back a week."

"As it is, you have slept two days," Tiaf declared.

"Two days?" Scott cried. "You mean I was unconscious two whole days?"

"You came from a great distance," Tiaf reminded Scott. Wichita was better than two hundred miles away. "And you were hurt. Teleportation requires energy. As does conversion. You will be very tired for a time."

"Still, I guess it's a small price to pay, Tiaf. I saved those kids."

"Yes," the old man agreed with a scowl. "At great danger."

"My ribs are well now."

"There are many types of danger," Tiaf grumbled as he passed his hand over a nearby viewing screen. Suddenly the image of an evening newscast appeared. A woman described the accident in detail, then spoke to the policeman who had tried to coax Scott from the corner.

"He seemed to know what was going to happen," the

officer declared. "It's spooky, ma'am. He was standing right under that sign when the whole mess broke loose and crashed down. I was sure he was under it, but all we found was dust. It was like he up and disappeared."

The anchorwoman then flashed a sketch of Scott across the screen. Next she interviewed some of the children, a few shoppers, even an old woman who was convinced Scott was the ghost of her dead son come back to warn of peril.

"It's dangerous, this kind of exposure," Tiaf said as he cleared the screen. "It draws interest. There is never a time when we Antrians can relax our caution."

No, Scott thought. Or be ourselves.

Scott passed the rest of the day in the tiny sleeping cubicle, drifting in and out of a peaceful rest. The next day he resumed his studies in the control room of the elongated cylinder which had brought Tiaf from a dying world to Earth a century earlier. That sterile, metallic world was now Scott's home as well.

For months Scott had labored to understand the various systems that guarded and operated the ship. The viewing screens were easiest. He simply focused his thoughts and projected them on the screen. In a matter of minutes he could gaze at visual projections of his very own thoughts.

"It's like inventing your own movie and seeing it in front of your eyes," Scott had told Tiaf the first time he had flashed a fantasy across the screen.

"Use caution, Scott," Tiaf had urged. "Your projections can take three-dimensional shapes as well."

And indeed they had. When a gang of curious boys

15

had approached the cave where the ship was hidden a month earlier, Scott had produced a pack of fierce dogs to send the intruders on their way. The only trouble had been in erasing the prowling creatures afterward.

"It's all mental discipline," Tiaf scolded. "Better to master your skills before projecting monsters onto the land."

Scott was half tempted to project a three-headed dragon or a prehistoric mammoth when the boys returned with their fathers. Instead, Tiaf had moved the ship elsewhere.

I'll do that, too, in time, Scott promised himself. It was the single skill that continued to elude him. By now he understood the workings of the solar cells lining the ship's exterior walls. They produced the power that energized the two massive electromagnets that locked onto energy fields and pulled the ship from one place to another. To focus the magnetic drive, a telepath required enormous concentration, and so far Scott had managed to move the ship only a few miles.

He'd had better luck with the dimensional drives. In addition to moving across surface distances, the cylinder, by means of accelerating rings outside its hull, could travel great distances in time and space. It was as though the secrets of the universe were at his fingertips.

But though Scott could feel his way through the stars or visit other times, he still couldn't drive the ship more than a mile or so across the hills of western Oklahoma.

"It's all a matter of concentration," Tiaf said over and over.

16

"But I *am* concentrating," Scott argued.

"Then maybe my calibrations are wrong," Tiaf declared as he played with dials on the control panel. Scott would again don the control bonnet and try to focus his thoughts on the desired movement. So far all was futile, though.

"I'll never catch on," Scott grumbled that night after another unsuccessful try.

"It's just another step up the ladder," Tiaf explained. "You have come so far in such a short time. Don't grow discouraged."

It was hard not to be disappointed. He was, after all, little better than a prisoner inside that giant tin can of a ship. Only when Tiaf guided the ship to a new destination did Scott take any real interest. In a small storage room aft Scott hid souvenirs of each place they visited. There were leaves of trees, and rocks chipped from granite hillsides or plucked from roaring creeks. On time excursions, Scott often collected coins or newspapers. To his dismay the coins often grew tarnished, and the newspapers yellowed or disintegrated entirely.

His favorite relics included a Persian vase and a Roman dagger. And, of course, the strangely lettered emerald ring.

The ring, Tiaf reminded Scott daily, was to amplify his thoughts. In time it would become unnecessary. To Scott that ring was a link with the dead Antrian world of his origins and a reminder of who he had become.

That night, as he lay alone in his sleeping cubicle, staring at the cold, sterile, metallic glow of the ceiling, Scott wondered how different things would have been had Tiaf never found him. Scott Childers might have remained an ordinary boy in a simple Texas town, who enjoyed staring at stars without really knowing why.

But then those kids would all be dead, Scott thought. Tiaf was right to find me, to teach me. We're messengers, we Antrians. We see dangers and offer warnings.

It's a wandering sort of life, though, Scott told himself. Sometimes you can almost fool yourself into being happy. Then the loneliness sets in.

Tiaf appeared in the doorway, and Scott knew he'd let his thoughts wander. A telepath often sees and hears everything, and Scott's deep wonderings and doubts must have burdened the old man fiercely.

"You feel the loneliness, too, don't you?" Scott asked.

"Before you came to me, I was the emptiest of all beings, a teacher without pupils, a guide without companions."

"So now we've got each other," Scott said, forcing a smile onto his face.

"Yes, but I wish you had a companion your own age," Tiaf confessed. "One with whom you could share your doubts and fears."

"Maybe I should create one," Scott said, grinning at the notion.

"That would never work," Tiaf said sadly. "You would need to direct his every thought, and there would be no surprise, no sharing of discovery."

"Is that so important?"

"Yes," Tiaf declared.

18

"Then perhaps we should find another town, a smaller one. I could try going to school, and—"

"We've tried that before, Scott. Look what happened in Wichita."

"I'll be more careful. I'll leave the ring behind. Maybe we can go into the mountains, to Wyoming or even Utah."

"And when you see danger? What will you do?"

"I don't know," Scott confessed. "Maybe I'll be able to close off my mind. I'm learning so much. Telepaths can control what they see and hear, can't they?"

"Perhaps. But a seer will always have visions, Scott. You will have them. What will you do? Act?"

"Maybe it won't be little kids this time. I couldn't let that boy with the red cap get crushed by a stupid sign, could I?"

"And afterward, when the others gather around and ask how you knew?" Tiaf asked. "When doctors come to examine your eyes and scan your organs?"

"I'll mask myself. We can conceal our ship. I can conceal myself."

"Can you? Your friends will ask, too. They will begin to wonder. Then they will grow suspicious. Why don't you live in the center of town like they do? Why don't you have brothers or sisters? Your parents are never around. Others will begin to call you names. In the end it's always the same. Better to stay where it's safe."

"Even if it's lonely?"

"I will try to be a better companion," Tiaf promised.

19

"You're my teacher," Scott said, nodding to the old man. "And my friend. You've taught me so much."

"But still you wish to venture forth among the Earthers," Tiaf said with a sigh. "It's the blood of Cilog, your father, which speaks. He, too, was an explorer. It's your nature, I suppose. But I fear what will happen."

"I have to try," Scott explained.

"Then tomorrow we will set out again, my young friend."

"Yes," Scott agreed, closing his eyes and drawing the wool blanket against his chin. The lights dimmed, and Scott heard the soft rustling sounds that marked Tiaf's departure.

Tomorrow we try again, Scott thought as he sought to envision what would come with the rising of the sun. No image appeared, though. Instead sleep captured his thoughts, and a rare peace settled over him.

3

Scott sat alone at the small metal table in the narrow room where he and Tiaf took their meals. The cylindrical design of the ship provided little enough space for its two occupants, and the galley, what there was of it, doubled as a study.

Scott gazed down at a map of southern Kansas. He was fond of making plans before setting out on a new project. Before leaving for Wichita, he had nearly memorized the street names, and he'd read and reread a guidebook. But in the end, it hadn't mattered.

If only that sign . . .

Scott erased the image of the crashing sign from his mind. Instead he studied the map. Wichita had been a failure. Cities were too full of dangers. A small town was better. But the map was speckled with towns. Which one?

Trust your senses, Tiaf always advised.

And so Scott closed his eyes and ran his fingers

along the map. Suddenly an image flooded his mind. He saw a broad yellow wheatfield cut by a narrow lane. A large, two-story house took shape beside the road. Other buildings rose from a nearby hill. In the center of the town stood two brown brick buildings. To one side, children chased one another around a playground. Their older brothers and sisters collected on the steps of the larger building. Over their heads CLEARMONT HIGH SCHOOL was engraved over the large double doors.

"Clearmont," Scott mumbled, opening his eyes. His finger rested atop that very town on the map.

"So, you've chosen," Tiaf said, glancing in through the narrow doorway.

"Yes," Scott said. "Clearmont. You'll move the ship?"

Tiaf nodded. Scott rose to his feet and followed the white-haired old man along to the control room. They sat alongside each other in the twin seats while Tiaf filled the viewing screen with the image of Clearmont, Kansas. The ship shuddered as the revolving rings outside hummed into motion. There was an abrupt jolt, and Scott felt himself grow numb. The world around him blurred, and the cylinder seemed to dissolve. In the blink of an eye, the ship split dimensions, then rematerialized at the edge of the wheatfield on the outskirts of Clearmont.

"What will it be this time?" Tiaf asked as he rose groggily to his feet. "Another cave? A barn perhaps?"

"A house," Scott said, filling the viewing screen with the picture of the two-story structure from his vision. "See, Tiaf? You can do it, can't you?"

"You can," Tiaf said, grinning. "Concentrate. Now."

Scott closed his eyes and focused on the house. Outside, walls began to enclose the ship. Windows and doors took shape. Rooms and a roof followed. Then Scott added carpets and furniture until the house seemed as much a home as any he'd ever known.

"What now?" Scott asked as he found himself standing on the landing of a broad staircase.

"The school?" Tiaf asked, joining him.

"Yes," Scott agreed. He stared at the emerald ring, then closed his eyes. In an instant he vanished.

Scott reappeared outside the ancient oaken door of the high school principal's office. The halls were deserted, and Scott knew school had yet to open. He took a deep breath, then opened the door and stepped inside. A small, dark-haired woman in a dark blue dress gazed up from a desk and nodded.

"New?" she asked.

"Yes, ma'am," Scott replied.

"I'm Mrs. Gardner, the school secretary," the woman explained. "Have a seat, young man, and I'll be right with you."

Scott sat on the edge of a bench and waited. Mrs. Gardner finished jotting something in a notebook, then waved Scott to her desk.

"Do you intend to enroll?" she asked.

"Yes, ma'am," Scott answered. "I just moved to Clearmont."

"Oh?"

"My . . . uncle . . . bought that big two-story house on the edge of town."

Mrs. Gardner scratched her head in confusion. Scott placed the image of the house in her head, though, and she smiled.

"Of course," she told him. "Your uncle should have come with you, though. We'll need—"

"I brought everything with me," Scott said. He concentrated on the ring, and a notebook appeared.

"Well, he should at least have called. Name?"

"Scott . . . Stone."

"Scott, we'll need a birth certificate to start with. Then a report card from your previous school, vaccination documents, and, of course, there are forms to fill out."

Scott nodded, then opened his notebook. By concentrating on blank sheets of paper, he was able to produce each required item.

"You appear a bit young for high school, Scott. This report card reads grade 9," the secretary noted.

"I've always been a little small for my age," Scott explained. "If you want, I could take a test."

"Oh, I don't think that will be necessary. Still, if your uncle were here, it would be much easier. Perhaps I could call him."

"Isn't it all there?" Scott asked, nervously shifting his feet as Mrs. Gardner shuffled papers. "We haven't got a phone."

"Oh, I see," Mrs. Gardner commented as she examined each document in turn. "Everything does seem to be here. I admit to being a bit surprised. You're unusually well prepared. Do you move around often, Scott?"

"Yes, ma'am," he said, fighting the urge to explain exactly how often.

"Let me leave you some forms to complete. Meanwhile, I'll take your papers to Mrs. Hunt, our counselor. She'll put a schedule together for you."

"Thanks," Scott said, taking the forms as Mrs. Gardner headed toward a door on the left. He took out a pen and began completing the forms. There seemed to be a thousand questions, and he nearly panicked. After all, he couldn't remember the birth date or place he'd imprinted on the transformed birth certificate, and he could hardly list his uncle as Tiaf! In the end, he closed his eyes and inscribed the forms with the identical answers printed on the other forms. Tiaf became T. F. Stone, and Mrs. Gardner, upon her return, appeared satisfied.

"Your first class will be English, Scott," Mrs. Gardner told him. "That's room 120, the far end of the south hall. One word of advice. Don't expect everyone to warm up to you right away. Clearmont is a small town, and most of the kids here have known each other forever. It may be hard fitting in for a while. Be patient. I know every boy and girl in this school, and there's not a really bad one in the bunch. Just a few who'll try your patience."

She concluded by waving him to the door with a smile, and Scott slipped out into the hall only seconds before a bell clanged loudly on the wall alongside. The front doors flew open, and a hundred or so high schoolers hurried inside. Scott dodged the first rush, then wove his way through the others down the hall toward room 120.

Mrs. Freer, the English teacher, greeted his arrival with raised eyebrows.

"Freshman?" she asked.

"Yes, ma'am," Scott assured her. As she examined his schedule card, he half wished he'd transformed himself a bit, added three or four inches at least.

But then I wouldn't be me anymore, he thought. There had, after all, been enough changes in his life. He had a new name, new home, even a new school now. Something ought to remain of the old Scott.

"We're just completing the study of clauses," Mrs. Freer explained as a crowd of curious classmates collected around Scott. "Tomorrow we have a test. Do you think you will need some extra study time?"

"No, ma'am," Scott told her. "I was in advanced studies back in . . . at my old school."

The teacher nodded politely. The students scowled. One even whispered, "Got ourselves a midget genius, huh?"

Scott followed Mrs. Freer to her desk and took a pair of heavy textbooks. He then found his way to the back of the room and took an empty seat in the corner. The bell announced the start of first period then, and Scott felt two dozen pairs of eyes examine every inch of him. Sneers and frowns answered his own shy grin.

He didn't attempt to participate in class. He knew he'd made too many mistakes already. As if the advanced studies remark hadn't been bad enough, Scott was overdressed. The others wore canvas shoes, blue jeans, and T-shirts. A few wore boots and overalls. Scott looked like he'd just walked out of a Wichita store window.

The best way to make an enemy is to show up a kid, Joey Smallwood had once told Scott. He'd just proved it was true.

His second class was math, and he'd barely left the English room when a pair of broad-shouldered giants drew him aside.

"Math?" the first said, snatching his schedule. "That's upstairs, kid. Better hurry, too. Mr. Conway hates tardies."

"Oh?" Scott asked. The schedule assigned his second class to room 132. The two boys scribbled new numbers for each class, though, then conducted Scott toward the stairs.

"See you later, kid," the taller one said. The other laughed.

Scott climbed the first two steps, then cautiously retraced his tracks. By hurrying along, he managed to slip through the door of room 132 seconds ahead of the bell.

"Mr. Conway, I'm Scott Stone," Scott told a tall man dressed in a white shirt and striped tie. "I'm new."

"Fine, Scott," the teacher said as he glanced at Scott's schedule. "I see someone's been kind enough to renumber your schedule. It's nice to see some of our students haven't lost their creativity. Shame they don't exhibit the same degree of imagination on their science

27

projects. Take the seat next to Lauren, over on the left. Lauren, see if you can repair Scott's schedule."

A slender girl with reddish blond hair and a thousand freckles motioned Scott toward an empty desk, and he headed there. Mr. Conway then supplied Scott with a textbook and several mimeographed sheets of class rules and study questions.

"Now, let's get on with geometry, people," the teacher called. The class grumbled, but hands reluctantly opened books, and the lesson commenced.

Scott did his best to avoid attention, but Mr. Conway wouldn't cooperate. He had each of the twenty students in the class solve problems on a graph board, and Scott's turn came quickly. Math had never been much of a challenge for him, and he almost scribbled the solution without thinking. He paused just in time. He scratched his head a minute, then cautiously located the points on the graph and connected them. He was tempted to miss the problem intentionally, but he feared being judged stupid and put back in eighth grade or assigned an easier class.

"Good, Scott," Mr. Conway said when Scott handed over the chalk. "I believe you may be able to keep pace with us."

"I hope so," Scott answered.

That comment drew a more favorable response from his classmates, and Lauren even smiled.

In truth, his ease at working through the material impressed her. When the bell dismissed class, she drew him aside.

"I'm Lauren Logan," she said. "It looks like we share several classes."

Scott handed over his schedule, and she rewrote the smudged room numbers.

"Thanks," he said when she returned the card.

"Next is art. Coming?"

"Sure," he said, hurrying along after her. Once in the hall, they avoided a throng of older students and made their way down a side hall past the cafeteria. That wing of the building obviously held the junior high classes, and smaller kids scurried past them. One, a freckle-faced boy of thirteen, skidded past Scott and hid behind Lauren's shoulder.

"Dale?" Lauren asked, turning to face the boy. "What's the matter with you?"

"Look!" the fearful boy answered, pointing down the hall at a gangling sixteen-year-old pounding his way toward them.

"My brother, Dale," Lauren explained to Scott. "That's Arthur Turner, resident pain."

"What'd you call me?" Turner asked, folding his hands across his stomach and staring icily at Lauren.

"You heard me," she barked. "Can't you find anything better to do than bully little kids?"

"He owes me money!" Turner insisted.

"Do not," Dale claimed. "Mr. Howland told you to leave us be. We don't have to give you anything."

"Howland isn't here," Turner said, shoving Scott to one side, Lauren to the other, and then clamping a firm hand on Dale Logan's scrawny neck. "Well, Logan?"

"Leave him alone!" Lauren cried, hurrying to her brother's defense. Scott caught his breath and tried to intercede.

"You'd better back away, friend!" Turner warned, shoving Scott aside a second time.

"Run, Dale!" Lauren called as she kicked Arthur Turner sharply in the shin. The bully howled in discomfort, and Dale scampered away. Lauren grabbed her books and tore off in the opposite direction. Only Scott remained.

"I'm going to enjoy this," Turner said, grabbing Scott's head in a hammerlock and dragging him into the boy's rest room across the hall.

"Let go," Scott pleaded as his books slipped from his fingers. "Let go!"

Inside the bathroom, junior highers spotted Turner and escaped to the hall. Older boys stared at Scott's contorted face and laughed. Scott struggled to breathe, fought to get his fingers around the ring, but it wasn't possible. Arthur Turner kicked open the first stall, and a startled twelve-year-old barked a challenge. The boy's face paled as Turner slapped the wooden wall with a free hand. The boy fled, and Turner dragged Scott inside. While a dozen onlookers watched, Turner pulled Scott's belt from his trousers, then bound Scott's hands behind the toilet.

"See you don't mess with me again, kid!" Turner warned as he slammed the door shut on his prisoner. And though Scott called for help, only laughter answered his pleas.

What a way to begin a new life! Scott thought as the bell rang, marking him tardy to third period. The rest room grew silent, and Scott suddenly felt desperately alone. He moved his fingers around so that they touched the strange green ring. Then, closing his eyes, he envisioned the hallway outside.

For a moment nothing happened. It was as if all Scott's strength had been sapped. He opened his eyes, blinked away a tear of rage, then concentrated harder. There was a flash of light, and he was gone.

4

Scott rematerialized in the doorway seconds later. As he recovered his senses, an astonished Dale Logan rushed to his side.

"How'd you get loose?" Dale asked. "I heard the guys. They tied you up in the bathroom. Nobody gets away from Art Turner."

"Oh, I've got a few tricks," Scott answered as he picked his scattered books off the floor.

"I guess so," Dale said, shaking his head.

"We better get to class now," Scott said, motioning Dale along. "Know where the art room is?"

"Sure," Dale answered, matching Scott's smile. "Follow me."

Scott hurried along after the speeding eighth grader, and in less than a minute they arrived at the art classroom. Scott nodded to Dale, then walked inside. After apologizing for being late, Scott took a vacant seat across a table from Lauren.

He said nothing to anyone about his encounter with Arthur Turner. He didn't need to. At lunch, standing in the cafeteria line behind Lauren, he couldn't help noticing the mixture of curiosity and wonderment that filled the gawking eyes of Dale Logan and his eighth-grade friends.

"You made a friend," Lauren whispered. "Scott Stone, champion defender of eighth graders."

"Sure," Scott mumbled. "You're the one who took up for your brother. Me, I only got trashed in the bathroom."

"I heard about that," she said, laughing. "How did you get loose so fast? I know you didn't get any help. Everybody enjoys seeing the new kid miserable."

"Everyone?" Scott asked.

"Well, just about," she replied. "Anyway, you seem to have wriggled your way out of trouble. Just watch out for Turner."

"I will."

Once they got their lunches—platters of thin roast beef, a scoop of mashed potatoes, and some green beans—Scott followed Lauren to a table in the back of the cafeteria. Moments later Dale and two companions arrived.

"One of the problems with having first lunch," she whispered to Scott. "Little brothers can be like gnats. You can't get shed of 'em no matter how hard you try."

She then rose to her feet, glared at the boys and cried, "Get!"

The three thirteen-year-olds scattered, and Scott laughed.

"Tagalongs," Lauren complained. "Would you believe it? I've got three of them altogether. Dale's the best. Once I get out of school, I'm cursed with tending the others, too."

"All brothers?"

"Yes," she grumbled as she cut a slice of beef and twirled it on her fork. "Dale, Drew, and Donny. Sometimes I wish we'd have a tornado, and they'd be gobbled up by the funnel cloud. It gets so tiresome, having them in your hair, never having a moment of peace or privacy. They go through my room when I'm not home! They spy on my friends and listen to my phone calls! Lord, I'm going to strangle all three of them one of these days."

"No, you won't," Scott said sadly. "You take up for them, too. Little brothers can be pests, but it's nice having somebody look up to you. There's a kind of glow in their eyes. You know they'll always see you just a little better than you really are."

"Yeah?"

"And even when they bug you to help solve math problems when you'd rather watch TV, you don't really mind. Not deep down anyway."

"You seem to know a lot about it."

"It's how it's always been with me and Brian," he explained. He said nothing more. Instead he scooped food into his mouth and tried to ignore Lauren's questioning eyes.

"Brian's your brother?" she asked when he finished. "How old?"

"Twelve."

"Seventh grader, huh? That's worse than eighth. Is he around? I'd like to meet him."

"We were really close," Scott said, fighting to erase Brian's face from his mind.

"Were?" Lauren asked.

"Yeah," he said somberly. "There was an accident, you see. A few months ago. Now, well, I live with my uncle."

"I'm sorry," she said, frowning. "You're right. I'd hate for anything to happen to Dale."

"It's hard being the only one left," Scott told her. "Harder than you can imagine."

"Sure," she agreed, brightening. "Come on. The bell's about to ring, and I know a shortcut to history."

They retrieved their books from a long line of shelves, and Scott followed her toward a side door. They flew past a dozen others when the bell announced the end of the lunch period. When they arrived at the history classroom, Scott showed the teacher, Mr. Edwards, his schedule, got a textbook, and took an empty desk in the far back corner of the room. A cloud of memories was descending on him, and he fought to escape them by concentrating on the industrial revolution.

Scott was on his own fifth period. He made his way to the gym for P.E. Coach Brewer, the instructor, grumbled about having another student, gave Scott a list of required equipment, then assigned him the duty of marking roll and copying the week's absentees on an office form.

"Tomorrow bring your shorts," the coach warned. "You'll get tired of paperwork. I do."

Scott thought he caught a trace of a grin in the hard-boiled face of Coach Brewer. And when the sixty-odd boys in the P.E. class arrived, Scott understood why a new boy wasn't exactly met with open arms. The class was made up of assorted sizes and shapes of boys. From scrawny seventh graders to a few sophomores and even a junior, the class was a cross section of Clearmont. And worst of all, in the center of the front row sat Arthur Turner.

Not a good sign, Scott thought as he located the missing boys on the seating chart. He then took out the hand-scrawled lists of absent boys and copied them onto Coach Brewer's gradebook. In no time at all Scott had finished. He then filled out the report and trotted over to the coach.

"All through," Scott said as his assembled classmates concluded their warm-up exercises.

"That fast?" Coach Brewer asked. "Son, I believe you'll do."

The coach then handed Scott a whistle and sent him off to referee the junior highers' basketball game.

For the first time in a long while Scott felt useful. More than that, he sensed a degree of belonging in spite of the younger boys' protests about his fairness. When the game was over, Dale Logan even gave Scott a halfhearted jab in the side.

"You make a lousy ref, Stone," Coach Brewer observed when Scott handed over his whistle in the coach's small office. "But you'd make a top-notch clerk. Bring your shorts tomorrow. Let's see what kind of player you are."

"Pitiful, I'm afraid," Scott confessed.

"We'll find something you can do. Now get out of here."

"Yes, sir," Scott said, darting outside. By the time he'd caught his breath and collected his books, the bell rang starting the sixth and final period. Scott hurried back to the main hall and made his way to the science lab.

"Survive P.E.?" Lauren asked, joining him beside the desk of Miss Ponds, the science teacher.

"Barely," he answered. "Tomorrow I'll have my gear, though."

"Oh, that'll make everything better," she said, sighing.

Scott nodded, handed the teacher his schedule, then waited for her to assign a seat and a book.

"I understand from Mrs. Hunt you were involved in an astronomy course at your previous school," Miss Ponds said as she gave Scott his biology text. "You're interested in the stars, I take it?"

"Used to be," Scott said. "We had a club, and we used to observe meteor showers, that sort of thing."

"Well, I want you to tell me about it one of these days, Scott. I've thought of starting an astronomy club here. I have a telescope at my home. Maybe you'd like to see it sometime?"

"Yes, ma'am," Scott said.

"Miss Ponds, I'm kind of showing him around," Lauren then said. "Do you suppose he could sit next to me for a while?"

"Tell Danny to move over one place," the teacher

suggested. "Just see you don't get to chattering away in my class."

"Yes, ma'am," Lauren promised, dragging Scott along to a row of lab tables near the center of the room.

Scott half smiled. But when class began, he focused his every attention on Miss Ponds and the lesson. He noted each word, but he never raised his hand. It was time to lie low, and he made himself as invisible as possible that final hour. When the bell rang, he gathered his belongings and hurried outside.

"Hold up there!" Lauren cried, racing after him. "What's the big hurry?"

"No hurry," he said, pausing to let her catch up. "I've got to get along home. My uncle—"

"Mom's bringing the van to pick us up," Lauren argued. "We'll drop you."

"I don't know," Scott said nervously.

"I do," she said, leading him toward the parking lot. "No normal person walks when he can ride. I admit you'll have to be pestered by three brothers, and Mom'll probably have a hundred questions, but it's worth not walking."

"I guess," Scott said, reluctantly agreeing. After all, how could he explain he had no intention of walking, that there was another method of transportation available?

Lauren's mother was waiting in the parking lot. Dale stood beside the cargo door of the Dodge van, waving both arms to attract his sister's attention. Scott waved back. Lauren only grumbled about little brothers and conducted Scott along.

"Mom, this is Scott Stone," Lauren said when they arrived. "Can we drop him off at his house? He's new here, and it's not too far out of the way."

"Where do you live, Scott?" Mrs. Logan asked.

Scott felt an icy chill creep through him. What was the address? He remembered writing it on the registration forms.

"Don't you even know where you live?" Lauren's youngest brother asked. "Even I know that!"

"Not much more than that, Donny!" Dale complained. "He just moved here."

"It's a big house at the edge of a wheatfield," Scott explained. "Route 5."

"That's a big help," Dale said, laughing. "Half the county's on Route 5. What road, Scott?"

"Cottonwood," Scott said, remembering. "Out on the edge of town."

"It's not far from us at all," Mrs. Logan said, smiling at Scott. "Of course, you'll have to ride in back with the menagerie."

"The what?" Donny asked.

"Never mind," Lauren said. "Donny, why don't you ride up front with Mom?"

The seven-year-old scrambled out of the van and raced around to the front seat. Lauren then led Scott into the cargo bay, and they sat together on a padded bench across from Dale and a younger, stone-faced brother of eleven.

"This is Drew," Lauren explained. "He's almost human. At least he doesn't make it his purpose in life to torment his sister."

"He's too busy being a genius," Dale commented. "Straight A's every report card. It's enough to make you sick."

"That's one sickness that ought to be contagious," Mrs. Logan declared as she started the car.

"I think that's great you make high marks," Scott told Drew. "I try hard myself, but I usually forget to do some assignment, or I put things off too long. Straight A's are hard to come by."

"Especially when you don't bring home your books," Lauren added, poking a finger into Dale's arm.

Dale scowled, but Drew brightened. The younger boy then began talking about his science fair project, and Scott was almost sorry he'd said anything. Lauren quickly turned the conversation into a travelogue, though. She pointed out the fire station, various stores, houses of friends and relatives.

"That's our place there," Dale cried, pointing out an attractive ranch-style brick house on Lawrence Street. Then Mrs. Logan turned onto Cottonwood.

"Strange, but I don't remember any houses out this way," she told Scott. "You're sure it's Cottonwood."

"Sure," Scott said nervously. He understood the method of projecting a mental image of the house, but Tiaf had never instructed how to explain the sudden appearance of a building where none had been before.

"You forget so much," Tiaf's voice spoke inside

Scott's mind. "Matter imprinting can change the memory as well, Scott."

The tall house loomed in the distance, and Scott hurriedly created a history for the place. It had belonged to T. F. Stone for twenty years. His grandfather, Franklin Stone, had built it. Scott then implanted the thought in the minds of the others.

"Of course," Mrs. Logan said, laughing to herself. "The Stone place. Your name is Stone, isn't it? I must be losing my senses."

"Too many boys," Lauren griped.

"Stone house?" Drew asked. "You sure? I don't remember it."

"You'd forget to put your pants on if nobody reminded you," Dale complained.

"I would not!" Drew objected.

Scott made his getaway as the two boys wrestled around the seat. Lauren hopped out and bid him goodbye.

"We could come by for you tomorrow morning," she offered. "It's not too far."

"Thanks, but it's better I get used to the walk," Scott told her. "My uncle says the exercise will be good for me."

"Sounds like Dad," Lauren muttered. "See you tomorrow."

"Bye," Scott told her. "Thanks for the ride, Mrs. Logan."

"Good-bye, Scott," the woman answered. Lauren's brothers waved their farewell, and the van made a U-

41

turn and headed homeward. Scott trotted up the walkway and entered the house.

"So, you survived one day," Tiaf called. "Is it what you hoped?"

"Not altogether," Scott admitted. "But I made a friend. And I feel almost normal."

"Normal?" Tiaf asked. "For an Earther?"

"Yeah, but I guess I'm not one, am I?"

"No, Scott."

"Still, I don't know what's normal for an Antrian, so maybe this is about as much as I can expect."

He then spread out his books on a table and began working a dozen geometry problems assigned for homework.

"Primitive mathematics," Tiaf said, glancing at the work. "You can do them in your head. We have studied geometric multiples, dimensional equations, and even astral geography."

"I know," Scott admitted. "Maybe it's too easy, but other kids are doing it. It doesn't hurt me, and it feels good. I'd almost forgotten about homework. Tomorrow I'll probably gripe about taking an English test, but right now I don't feel so different."

"Different isn't always bad," Tiaf pointed out.

"Maybe not, but it's sure hard." Scott then smiled as he completed the first graph.

"Perhaps," Tiaf whispered as he sat across the table. "It's good to see you smile. Lately there have been too many frowns."

"I know," Scott said, setting aside his pencil long

enough to gaze up at his companion. "You've taught me so much, Tiaf. But I'm just fourteen. I want to be with other kids."

"Yes," the old man said, nodding. "Use caution, though. You can look the same as the others, do as they do, but you will always be different. And that can prove dangerous."

Scott nodded, then resumed his homework.

5

The rest of the week passed in a blur of school assignments and new faces. Gradually the curious, sometimes hostile, glances of his classmates faded. They were replaced by amused nods or even an occasional grin. He began to feel comfortable—except in P.E.

"Don't try so hard," Coach Brewer urged after Scott missed his tenth straight shot in the daily basketball game. "Relax. Be patient."

It was hard, being patient. And things got no better the second week. The other players didn't make it any easier. "What do you expect?" Art Turner asked as he tossed the ball to his younger brother Chip. "Kid's got chicken legs!"

"Chicken legs," the others echoed.

"Hey, Chicken Legs, was your mother a hen or something?" Art asked.

Scott did his best to ignore their taunts, but the words cut through him like a well-honed blade. And yet whenever he stood his ground, he was generally bounced around more than the basketball.

"Sorry," the Turners would call when they shouldered Scott out of the way. "Didn't see you, Chicken Legs."

Scott scowled and picked himself off the floor. By week's end he had at least one bruise for each game.

"Chicken Legs," he grumbled as he followed Dale Logan to the showers. Scott felt as if every eye in the crowded locker room was fixed on those legs. "I'm not that skinny, am I?" he asked Dale.

"Pretty skinny," Dale told him. "Me, too. Mom says it's from talking, but it can't be. You barely say three words, Scott."

It's those protein pills of Tiaf's, Scott thought. Tiaf might implant the image of juicy steaks or thick pork chops, but it was, after all, just a few chemical compounds.

Maybe that was why when Lauren and Dale invited Scott to the neighborhood Dairy Queen Tuesday after school, he jumped at the chance. The place was crowded with teenagers, mostly freshmen and sophomores, with a few younger kids sprinkled in. The walls vibrated with music from an old-fashioned jukebox, and Lauren began singing along with a dozen others.

"This is as close as we get to entertainment around here," Dale said as he paid for three malts and waved Scott to a nearby booth. "Lauren usually goes a little crazy around here. Don't worry. She'll snap out of it eventually."

When the song was over, Lauren joined them in the

booth. She quickly set to work on her strawberry malt, and except for babbling out a few comments on the afternoon history quiz, she devoted herself entirely to drinking. Scott, on the other hand, was in no hurry. The thick drink brought back a flood of fond recollections, and each taste was like a trip backward in time, to a place that seemed lost to him nowadays.

"Know this one, Scott?" Lauren asked as a new song boomed out from the jukebox. "Want to sing with us?"

Scott shook his head sadly. Instead he grinned as Lauren joined the others in a humorous chorus, all about a girl determined to steal the heart of a guy named Larry.

"Hey, Chicken Legs!" Brad Parker called. "Don't you know how to sing?"

Scott glared. Brad was tall and muscular, a natural leader among the sophomore class. Always before he'd seemed sort of friendly.

Scott set aside his malt long enough to stand.

"I can sing," he told the others. "Only I'd hate to run everybody off. I sound about like that muffler on Art Turner's pickup."

The others laughed, and Brad said, "You're all right, kid."

"I've got a name," Scott pointed out.

"Yeah, Chicken Legs," Chip Turner added.

Scott didn't laugh, and neither did most of the others.

"Shut up, Turner," Lauren yelled. "Nobody's talking to you."

Brad flashed a warning glance in the direction of

shaggy-haired Chip, and the thirteen-year-old melted into the crowd.

"Nobody bothers with the Turners," Brad said, stopping briefly at Scott's booth. "I didn't mean anything, you know. You'll get used to us soon. We're kind of like a town of cousins here, and everybody rides somebody now and then."

"Sure," Scott said. "I do have skinny legs, I guess."

"Yeah, you do," Lauren agreed.

"At least you wash 'em," Dale added. "Those Turners—"

"Hey, they've got their troubles, too," Brad pointed out. "You ought to stay clear of them, Dale. Ever since their folks split up, Art's been real trouble. He failed last year, and then he got in a lot of trouble when you turned him in to the principal. Mr. Howland got onto him bad."

"Not enough," Dale complained. "He bullies the whole eighth grade! He's headed for reform school. Everybody says so."

"Just you make sure he doesn't murder you along the way," Lauren warned.

Brad and the others grinned. Scott took a long sip of malt.

"You know, we really ought to do something about those legs," Lauren said after Brad returned to the others. "And you're too pale for it to be March, Scott."

"Baseball tryouts are this week," Dale declared. "How old are you?"

"I'll be fifteen this summer," Scott told them.

"Then you can try out for the Zoo League," Dale explained.

"The what?" Scott asked.

"Zoo League," Lauren answered. "See, all the teams have animals for mascots. Bears, Lions, Tigers, Hawks . . . you get the idea. It's really the Junior Commercial League. Fourteen and under."

"I'm really awful at baseball," Scott warned.

"Worse than basketball?" Dale asked.

"Afraid so," Scott confessed. "Much worse."

"You may be in real trouble, Scott," Lauren said. "Nearly everybody in Clearmont plays spring baseball."

"Even me!" Dale added.

"Hey, don't let him con you," she said, elbowing Dale in the ribs. "He's a terror on a ball field."

"Dynamite second baseman," Dale boasted. "Anyway, I can work with you, help you learn how to field and hit. Lauren's a fair pitcher."

"You play?" Scott asked.

"Not anymore," she answered shyly. "Three brothers are enough sport for anybody. I like to watch, though."

"That I can do, too," Scott pointed out. "Without making a fool out of myself, either."

"Oh, you've got to try," Dale urged. "You could use the exercise, and even if you strike out every time you're up, the kids will get to know you."

"He's right," Lauren insisted.

"You don't know," Scott told them. "I played Little League when I was nine. It's a miracle I survived. I was terrible."

"We've got till Friday," Dale reminded Scott. "Get your glove, and we'll meet you after supper at your place. There's plenty of space out there. Leave everything else to me."

Scott gazed in wonder at Dale's confident face. The younger boy was suddenly transformed. Lauren's eyes pleaded, too, and Scott reluctantly agreed. He then gulped the last of his malt and followed his friends outside.

Back home he thought better of his decision. He was tempted to produce a phone and call Lauren with some excuse.

"They're right," Tiaf told him. "If you truly want to be one of them, you have to join in their games."

"I do," Scott insisted. "But baseball! I used to have nightmares about that. And besides, I don't have any equipment."

"What do you need?"

Scott began to make a list, but Tiaf halted him. Instead the old man turned away a moment and began producing each item. First a leather glove appeared. Then balls and bats. Scott half believed Tiaf would have built a domed stadium outside.

"Is there anything you can't produce?" Scott cried in disbelief.

"Yes," Tiaf said, gently touching Scott's shoulder. The old man's fingers trembled slightly, and Scott sighed.

"I haven't been around much, have I?" he asked. "I've neglected my lessons. I promise, Tiaf, once this baseball business is over, I'll work hard. Saturday we can devote the whole day to working."

"Only when you are ready," Tiaf explained. "Even on Pyto boys had their holidays."

Scott grinned, then took the glove, bats, and balls back to his room. He got into a pair of ragged jeans and slipped an old sweatshirt over his bony shoulders. By the time Lauren and her brothers arrived, Scott was ready to join in the game.

He was every bit as bad as he'd warned. The ball eluded his glove more often than not, and the bat felt awkward in his hands. Before, at least he'd felt comfortable. Now every motion seemed foreign. He tripped when trying to field ground balls, and he seemed unable to judge the flight of a pop-up.

"He really is bad," Drew observed. "Worse than Donny."

Scott tossed his glove aside and sat down, totally defeated.

"Hey, get up!" Dale yelled. "Friday's a long ways off."

But though Scott worked at it each afternoon, he improved only slightly. And when Friday arrived, he wished he were sick.

"You'll do all right," Dale assured him. "You're hitting the ball fair now, and if you remember to block the ball with your body, then toss the ball to first nice and easy, you'll do fine."

Scott wasn't so sure. And as he watched the other boys toss baseballs in an easy motion or slap pitches into the outfield, he was more discouraged than ever.

"Where'd you dig this glove up, anyway?" Chip Turner asked as Scott picked up a bat and prepared to hit. "Mickey Mantle autograph? This must've been your grandpa's."

"Maybe," Scott said sourly. "It does the job, though."

"Better'n you," Chip added, and the others laughed.

Scott might have barked an angry answer, but in truth, Chip Turner was right. Scott proved so when he hit the first pitch weakly to the shortstop. Scott was barely out of the batter's box when the ball popped into the first baseman's mitt.

"You're out!" the umpire called.

Scott turned and retreated to the bleachers.

"Chicken Legs strikes out again!" Chip called.

"Grounded out!" Scott objected.

Scott would have happily quit that very moment, but the coach called for him to take a second try. Chip Turner raced out to the infield and took the place of the third baseman. Scott tried to cast the taunts of the others from his mind, but they plagued him like a swarm of hornets. Then, suddenly, his mind cleared.

"Use your vision," Tiaf whispered. "Trust your sight."

Scott concentrated on the pitcher, gripped the bat, and waited for the pitch. The ball flew toward the plate, and Scott's arms exploded into motion. The bat whacked the ball and sent it burning right at Chip Turner. The third baseman dove to the ground as the ball flew overhead and on into left field.

"Run, Scott!" Dale screamed, and Scott charged to-

51

ward first base. He made a careful turn, then headed for second. He might have gone on to third but his toe caught the corner of the bag at second base, and Scott tumbled earthward. He only barely managed to scramble back to second base before the shortstop applied a tag.

"Good hit!" a burly man Dale had pointed out as Amos Gladbury's father called out. "Take left field, son."

Scott nodded, then trotted back to get his glove. Dale tossed it to him near third base.

"Sorry I'm such a klutz," Scott told Mr. Gladbury as he headed for the outfield.

"Just a little too excited is all," the coach answered. "Remember, cut everything off and throw to second."

Actually, though, Scott had only one chance to touch the baseball, and he missed that one. The ball bounded through Chip Turner's legs, and Scott raced after it. The ball outran him, though, and all he could do was chase it helplessly to the fence while the hitter circled the bases.

After the tryouts were over, Scott sat with Dale on a bench and sipped a root beer.

"I warned you," Scott said, trying to manage a smile.

"You weren't so bad," Dale remarked. "You hit a double."

"I was a disaster," Scott declared. "I tried, but I've never had much coordination. My head works just fine with figures, but I just wasn't born to be an athlete. My little brother had to teach me how to swim!"

"Lauren told me about your family. Sorry."

"Yeah. I used to wish I were more like Brian, more like you."

"Me?" Dale asked in surprise.

"Just one of the gang," Scott explained. "It's not much fun being different, always being the outsider."

"Oh, you'll get used to things. Everybody's got problems. Me, I'm a shrimp!"

"You'll grow," Scott assured him. "I'll never be any good at baseball."

Lauren joined them then.

"Well?" she asked. "How'd it go?"

"We'll find out Monday," Dale answered. "That's when the coaches will post the lists."

"Think I'll have somebody to cheer?" she asked, turning to Scott.

"Somebody," he answered. "Not me."

b

Scott waited until Saturday to share his feelings with Tiaf.

"Failing is always painful," Tiaf declared, "but to a seer, emotion cuts like a knife. You feel it deeper than others, so you must cast it aside."

"How?" Scott asked. "How do you forget something that hurts?"

"By replacing it with a better thought," the old man answered. "Or with studies."

Most likely the latter, Scott thought as Tiaf helped him into the ship's right-hand control chair.

"I leave you to practice your projections," Tiaf said as the viewing screen came to life. "I have some calibrations to complete."

"I promise to work hard," Scott said.

But once Tiaf departed the chamber, Scott let his mind wander. The screen allowed him to venture through time and space, across great distances, even journey into his own imagination if he so chose. In the beginning Scott contented himself with exploring the history of Clearmont. He watched the first cabins appear on the endless prairie, then saw buildings rise, a street paved, watched automobiles replace wagons.

Even better were more recent scenes. He slowed the screen's accelerated pace to watch Lauren. As a toddler she'd been as awkward as Scott, had wrecked her bike by running it into a culvert. Later, as she grew, Scott watched a new confidence, a poise of sorts, appear. He slowed the screen even more as it approached the current date. Days before Scott's arrival she'd sat alone in most classes, devoting her time and energies to her studies.

He'd expected her to be more relaxed, to have hundreds of friends. As he followed her through the school, though, he saw she laughed and chatted with everyone, but not in the same way she did with Scott.

Suddenly he saw himself enter English that first day. Her eyes took notice right away. Scott focused on her thoughts. He tried to discover her feelings, but he had no talent for breaking through mental barriers the way Tiaf did. Still, he could see well enough what she did, where she went. And after lunch, when Scott departed for the gym, his eyes followed Lauren toward the girls' changing room.

"Scott!" Tiaf cried just as the door swung open. The screen went blank, and Scott gazed sheepishly into the eyes of his tutor.

"I was . . . just . . . practiced my projections," he explained.

"Seers have a gift," Tiaf scolded. "The gift was never intended to allow intrusions."

"I've never tried before," Scott explained, his face reddening with embarrassment.

"Your mind can take you many places," Tiaf continued. "Some are to be avoided. Your talents should lead to understanding and knowledge."

"That's where they were headed," Scott said, laughing nervously. "I'm sorry, Tiaf, but what do you expect? I'm just being a normal fourteen-year-old."

"Normal?"

"Like everybody else. Don't tell me boys on Pyto never projected a locker room."

"On Pyto, there were no secrets," Tiaf admitted. "But here, Scott, you creep into lives like a thief in the night. There's great danger in knowing too much. You search for love and belonging, but Earthers have no shielding against telepathy. Their thoughts wander aimlessly, and some of those thoughts will bring you great pain. Wait for their words, little friend."

"I was only curious," Scott explained. "I wasn't trying to probe minds."

"No?"

"Well, maybe I was looking into Lauren's."

"Scott, if you break down the barriers your own senses have erected, you will find yourself beset by a thousand thoughts. Seers can suffer a profound madness if bombarded by so many undisciplined minds."

56

"I'll be more careful," Scott promised. "I was, after all, only going to take a peek. Like anybody would."

"Anybody?" Tiaf quizzed. "Everybody? Scott, you aren't anyone or everyone. You'll always be different. Don't forget. You weren't born to this world."

"I know, but maybe I can be one of them if I try really hard."

"Like at the baseball field?" Tiaf asked, raising an eyebrow.

"I won't always do so poorly," Scott declared. "I perform my schoolwork well. I'm treated like any other freshman."

"You put on a fine mask, Scott. But what will you do when another sign begins to fall? What will you do when you pass a child fated to drown?"

"Maybe that won't happen," Scott said, turning away as the image of a drowning boy flooded the screen.

"I know you too well, Scott. The vision will come, as it did in Wichita, in Clayville, in Morgantown and Tulsa. The visions will always come, and you will always heed them."

"I could change," Scott protested.

"Can you?" Tiaf asked. Skepticism filled the old man's eyes as he cleared the screen. Then Tiaf placed the control bonnet on Scott's head and completed the instrument adjustments.

"Time to work?" Scott asked.

"Yes," Tiaf declared. "Now, see if you can imprint your own image on the screen."

Scott concentrated, and his head took shape. His

shoulders followed. Then the rest of him appeared, at least down to the knees. Try as he might, though, Scott couldn't add the feet.

"They won't call me Chicken Legs now," Scott said, laughing. Instantly the image vanished, and Tiaf scowled.

"Concentrate," the tutor urged.

Scott tried again. This time the legs came first, but they weren't Scott's. Huge muscles bulged. Instead of the pale white coloring, the legs were tanned and leathery. Dark black hairs sprouted. Tiaf chuckled, and Scott suddenly felt something tickle his knees. Glancing down, he saw his own legs mirror the projected ones.

"Ahhh!" Scott cried. Instantly the screen went blank, and his legs returned to their normal state.

"Now, again," Tiaf instructed.

This time Scott was able to transmit his own image onto the screen. It was strange, watching himself.

"Now, what would you change?" Tiaf asked.

Scott stretched the figure a foot, then added muscle and a tan. Finally, almost as an afterthought, he imagined a heavy mustache.

"I look pretty good," Scott noted. "But it's not me," he added sadly. The picture faded, and Scott's old self reappeared.

"Is it so bad to be yourself?" Tiaf asked. "Now, remove the bonnet and try it again."

Scott concentrated. The helmet wasn't a lot of help except when teleporting objects. The screen itself read Scott's thoughts and translated them into pictures or action.

"If I can do all this without the bonnet, why bother with the thing?" Scott asked. "You never use yours."

"Because you cannot pilot the ship," Tiaf explained. "Until you can do that without the bonnet, it must be kept calibrated."

"Why? You're always here."

"Always is a contradiction unto itself," Tiaf declared. "No one, not Earther or Antrian, not even a seer, can be certain of everything."

"I guess," Scott admitted. "Still, it seems like a waste of time."

"We have nothing so much as we have time, Scott."

Yes, I know, Scott thought. Time crept so swiftly across Earth, but Tiaf seemed immune to its effects.

"Why should I age when I am the master of my molecular composition?" Tiaf asked. "I can be whatever I wish."

"Why didn't you come as a boy to me?" Scott asked. "I wouldn't be so lonely."

"You needed an elder," Tiaf explained as he instantly transformed himself into a second, smallish blond boy of fourteen. "You needed a guide, not a mere companion."

"Yes, I guess that's right, Tiaf," Scott admitted as Tiaf returned to his earlier appearance. "But now—"

"Perhaps you need both," Tiaf finished. "There is yet much to learn, Scott. Come. We will work on telekinesis."

Scott frowned and trudged along with his tutor. Telekinesis involved moving objects with the mind. It would allow him to take control of the ship. But of all the tasks Tiaf set before him, telekinesis was the single one Scott seemed unable to master.

"Here," Tiaf said, setting a small metallic disk on the table in the galley. "Focus your mind on it, Scott. Move it from one end of the table to the other."

Scott sat opposite the disk and concentrated. He placed his fingers on his temples and pressed, as if that would somehow strengthen his will. A humming sound vibrated through his ears, and he began to perspire.

Move, he silently told the disk. Move! But in spite of his every effort, the little metal circle remained glued to the tabletop. Scott drew his hand away and glanced at the ring.

"No!" Tiaf warned. "Use your mind, Scott!"

It was like the baseball tryouts all over again. Here was a task Scott was incapable of completing. Give him something easy, like a hundred equations to solve in half an hour. His mind would race through that sort of work. Telekinesis remained foreign, an unsolvable mystery.

"Concentrate," Tiaf said, placing his hands on Scott's tense shoulders. "Harder."

Scott felt tears roll down his cheeks as his head began to throb. His mind seemed to glow hot like the burner on a stove. He shuddered and ached. But as his eyes grew wider, the disk finally stirred.

"Harder," Tiaf urged.

Scott heard his teeth grinding against one another as he glared at the disk. It moved again, and again. Finally it fell from the corner of the table and rolled off across the floor. Scott tried to relax, but it didn't appear possible. Where his gaze fell, the table glowed white-hot.

"Blink your eyes, Scott," Tiaf suggested, and Scott did so. He then shook his head. The focus broke, and a tremendous pounding erupted inside his head.

"Tiaf?" Scott cried as he clasped his hands to his head. His mind felt as if it were splitting itself wide open.

"Close your eyes," Tiaf instructed as he held a sonic vibrator against Scott's neck. Sound waves began to fight the pounding while Tiaf's strong hands massaged Scott's tortured shoulders. A bright light seemed to send splinters of pain through Scott's mind. He cried out, tried to fight off the pain. Then, in the blink of an eye, the discomfort ceased. In its place came a cool, comforting shudder of relief.

Scott dropped his chin onto his chest. For a few moments he lost consciousness. When he regained his senses, he found Tiaf bathing his forehead with a sweet ointment.

"I thought my mind would explode!" Scott exclaimed. "Tiaf, the pain!"

"You crossed a barrier," the old man explained. "Here. Try to move the disk now."

Scott shook his head and backed away from the table. The staggering pain was too fresh a memory.

"Look at it," Tiaf commanded.

Scott glanced at the disk. In an instant it flew across the table.

"I don't understand," Scott said, shivering as the icy ointment penetrated his flesh. "How is it possible?"

61

"On Pyto your abilities would have grown as you aged. Here, you have been too long with others."

"I can move the ship now, can't I?"

"And much more," Tiaf declared proudly. "You must learn control, but it will come. Rest a few minutes. Then we will try a greater challenge."

Scott rested his head on the table. A shudder of relief ran through him. He closed his eyes, but instead of darkness, he saw himself piloting the ship through the stars, a celestial navigator like his true father. He smiled at the notion, but only for a second. Then he remembered Lauren, the school, his new friends.

"Come," Tiaf said then, leading Scott back to the pilot's seat of the craft. Scott took his place beside the tutor, and Tiaf turned the knobs so that new coordinates appeared on the guidance console.

"We can't," Scott objected. "What about the house?"

"It will appear as always," Tiaf explained. "Remember, we travel in less than an instant."

"Where?" Scott asked.

"To a distant place where no one will trouble us."

Scott thought to voice a complaint, but the ship lurched, and they were there already. Scott gazed at the screen, and a desolate canyon of high reddish walls appeared.

"There, see that rock?" Tiaf asked.

Scott gazed at a huge boulder on the far rim of the canyon. Suddenly it began rolling down the steep wall toward the ship.

"How do I move?" Scott asked. "It's coming right at us."

"Don't move the ship," Tiaf advised. "Deflect the rock."

Scott stared at the bounding boulder and fixed it in his mind. Instantly the rock shattered into a thousand harmless fragments.

"I did that?" Scott asked, shrinking into his chair.

"Yes," Tiaf answered, shaking his head. "Deflect, Scott. Not destroy."

A second boulder thundered toward the ship, and again Scott exploded it into bits.

"Deflect," Tiaf repeated, placing a firm hand on Scott's arm. "Don't merely focus on the rock. Fix in your mind what you would have it do."

Scott nodded. When a third rock rumbled down the canyon wall, Scott managed to change its course, defying the natural forces of gravity so that the rock tumbled harmlessly away from the ship.

"You are beginning to understand," Tiaf observed. "Just now you pose great danger to everyone, Scott. You must practice until your natural instincts are harnessed."

"Natural instincts?"

"When a danger approaches, you will always react against it. Without thinking, a seer may cause great injury. He must always consider his actions before responding."

"That seems more difficult than moving the disk."

"It is," Tiaf agreed. "Practice. Soon a new instinct will supersede the old one. You will have the power of telekinesis, but the danger will pass."

Scott nodded. More boulders, three this time, headed

for the ship, and he fought the urge to strike out blindly. He fixed each in his mind and turned it aside. The lesson went on and on until Scott found himself closing his eyes and envisioning the entire canyon. Without actually viewing the boulders, he deflected them away like so many tennis balls.

"Good," Tiaf proclaimed at last. "Now, guide us back to Clearmont."

"Drive the ship?"

"Yes, Scott. It's time."

Scott turned the dials so that the original coordinates reappeared. Then he closed his eyes and viewed the ship. Beneath him, the cylinder began to vibrate. Then, as light seemed to flash through the compartment, the ship returned to Clearmont.

7

Scott wanted to rush outside and tell the whole world
of his exploits. Whoever heard of a boy smashing boulders, deflecting rocks as easily as a baby wiggles his
toes? But there was no one to tell. He was tempted to
flash over to Lauren's house, but what use was that?
He could never tell her, not and stay.

"You have worked hard today," Tiaf said as Scott
rose from the chair and wiped his forehead. "Would
you like to use the viewing screen?"

"Sure," Scott said, gazing at the blank screen. Usually he delighted in journeying through time and space,
seeing distant lands and forgotten civilizations. But his
heart wasn't in it. Tiaf noticed immediately.

"You'd rather be playing baseball and sipping
malts," Tiaf observed.

"Angry?"

"No, it's only to be expected, after all. I know you
still miss your family."

Scott felt his knees wobble as he watched the screen. The image of the man and woman he'd always known as parents appeared. Beside them was the blond-haired wisp of a brother who would have howled with delight if Scott told of his encounter with the boulders.

"Maybe this summer we could take Brian with us," Scott said, turning with hopeful eyes toward Tiaf. "Just for a time. He'd tell no one. He'd be such good company."

Another figure floated across the screen. Sharon. They'd been friends since either one of them could remember. Scott smiled as he watched her walk slowly along the creek where they'd once spotted the first robin of spring. The smile faded when he realized she was headed toward the cemetery.

"You know it's impossible," Tiaf whispered. "Have you forgotten you're dead to them?"

"We could find a way," Scott said, shivering as he watched Sharon place flowers beside the simple brass plaque that read SCOTT CHILDERS. "Tiaf, you can do anything."

"It's far too dangerous," Tiaf warned. "For them as well as for you."

"One day I'll be able to go back, won't I?"

"How?" Tiaf asked. "Disguised as a stranger, perhaps to bring back to them all the pain they have felt thinking you gone? How could you keep silent seeing them? I know your heart aches even now, watching them."

Yes, Scott thought. He's right. After all, it's not so bad here.

"Perhaps," Tiaf responded. But Scott knew what the wise old man was thinking: Yes, it's not so bad now. But how long can it last?

The words haunted Scott the rest of the weekend. In his dreams he saw himself bidding Lauren farewell. He sat beside Tiaf as the ship vanished, taking with it the tall house and all recollection of the boy named Scott Stone.

That's how it's likely to be, too, Scott told himself as he dressed for school Monday morning. We can't leave questions behind to cause suspicion.

But by the time he'd arrived at the school, he'd managed to chase such gloomy thoughts from his mind. Dale Logan grabbed his arm and dragged Scott along to the gym door. Lists of players were taped there, and Dale fought his way through a crowd in order to search for his name.

"Falcons!" Dale cried, jumping in the air. "Fulton Bakery Falcons!"

"Don't fly away, Falcon," Scott pleaded. "Me?"

"Who, you?" Chip Turner asked. "Who'd take you, Chicken Legs?"

A wave of anger ran through Scott's mind, and it was all he could do to hold back an instinct to incinerate Chip's toenails.

"Dale?" Scott asked instead.

"They must've forgot to list you," Dale answered, studying the various sheets. "That's great. You can join the Falcons. Teams always need a few extra players."

"That's right," Bucky Hart said, and the other boys agreed.

"Thanks just the same," Scott said as he turned away.

"Come on, Scott," Dale said, racing around to block Scott's escape. "It'll be fun. You'll see."

"No, I think I used up all my athletic talents hitting that double," Scott argued. "I'll come watch you play, though. That's all I would have done anyway. This way Lauren can sit on the bench beside me."

"Yeah?" Dale asked, grinning.

"That all right with you?"

"Shoot, it's just fine. Truth is, I was worried she might never have a real boyfriend. The last one, a guy named George Kincaid, fell down a well shaft and drowned a couple of years back."

"Oh?" Scott asked.

"Shook her up pretty good. She didn't talk much for about a year. She's better now."

"Losing a friend can be hard," Scott explained.

"Guess not as bad as losing a whole family, though."

"No," Scott said, swallowing his sadness and hurrying toward the side door where Lauren was waiting.

"Well?" she asked.

"I'm a baseball washout," Scott informed her.

"Disappointed?"

"Some," he confessed. "And relieved. I would've made a lousy player, you know."

"I know," she admitted.

Before they could speak another word, the bell clanged, and Scott hurried inside the building.

The day went downhill from there. To begin with,

Mrs. Freer handed back English tests, and they spent the period discussing errors Scott hadn't made. In math Mr. Conway assigned a seemingly endless series of graph problems. Scott finished halfway through the period, and his classmates were none too pleased by that.

Fortunately Scott managed to get to art class without bodily injury. Mrs. Lyles gave them a free drawing period, and Scott took a pencil and began sketching.

His mind began to wander almost immediately. Maybe it was seeing Sharon at the graveyard, or perhaps viewing his parents and Brian. Possibly it had to do with the tale of George Kincaid, Lauren's dead friend. Whatever the reason, Scott's drawing set a strange star in the midst of a distant galaxy. It was a world Tiaf had often described, the Antrian sun and the colonies on the planet Pyto.

There was a stark realism to the sketch. It was hauntingly believable. And yet the world Scott drew had died before he had been born, scorched in a supernova that devoured everything in a gaseous whirl of flame.

"What in the world is that?" Lauren whispered as she peeked over his shoulder.

"Not in the world," he answered. "Beyond."

"Scott?"

"It's a star system light years away," he told her. Of course, it no longer exists, he should have added. My mother and father came from there. It's why I know things, why I can create report cards and deflect boulders. Because, Lauren, I'm not like you.

"Well, Scott, you've certainly used your imagination today," Mrs. Lyles commented as she looked at the drawing. "The sun, isn't it?"

"Yes, ma'am," Scott replied. *My* sun, he should have said.

"I'll bet Miss Ponds would like to see this. Would you allow me to show it to her?"

"Sure," Scott agreed.

"She's never seen the sun, huh?" Mark Carter asked.

"Not from close up like Scott has," Lauren added.

The others laughed at the thought, and Lauren shook her head angrily.

"You know what I mean," she complained. "He studied the sun and the planets at his old school. He took an astronomy class."

"Looks to me like he might have paid the place a visit," Lewis French observed. "Fly up there in the stars, do you, Scott?"

"All the time," Scott said, grinning.

The class laughed along, and Scott swallowed a shudder. If only they knew.

"You ask me, the kid's pretty weird!" Jesse Wiggins added. "Drawing stars!"

"Got to draw something," Teresa Brum declared. "Some people get tired of drawing Chevy pickups all the time."

The class laughed louder. It might have made Scott feel better another day, but more than ever he felt alone, shut off, different. Afterward, at lunch, he kept

70

to himself. He even turned down Dale's offer of a free cupcake.

Things got no better that afternoon. To begin with, he forgot his history book, and Mr. Edwards assigned a free reading period.

"Guess that's homework for you, Scott," the teacher declared.

P.E. was even worse. Coach Brewer was absent, and Mrs. Hunt, the counselor, took charge of the class. She was young, slightly built, and totally overwhelmed by the crowd of noisy boys filling the gym.

"What do you usually do when Coach Brewer's out?" she asked.

"Play dodgeball!" Art Turner shouted.

"Yeah!" the others agreed.

Scott was in no position to argue. He'd never known the coach to be out. Dale sighed.

"Dodgeball is just legalized slaughter," Dale told Scott. "Watch and see for yourself."

Scott couldn't help grinning. Some of the older boys divided the class, and Scott followed his captain to the far end of the gym. What followed was a mixture of chaos and brutality.

At first it wasn't so bad. There were so many bodies, it was hard to get a clear shot at anyone in particular. But as the ranks thinned, Art Turner and a pair of others zeroed in on Scott. Balls raced in like rockets, but Scott ducked and dodged. And when one ball in particular seemed destined to strike home, it suddenly veered away and slammed harmlessly against the wall.

"Good reflexes," Lewis French declared.

"Just my instinct for self-preservation," Scott explained.

Moments later Scott even managed to catch Turner himself with a well-placed shot. In seconds the first game was over.

That only marked the beginning of Scott's trouble. As balls flew across the gym, Scott's mind suddenly went blank. A dark black bank of clouds appeared. Thunder rumbled and a wicked yellow streak of fiery lightning erupted out of nowhere and blazed straight at . . .

It wasn't lightning that slammed against Scott's chin, though. Arthur Turner, never one to miss his chance, had fired a volleyball right at Scott's head. One minute Scott was standing between Dale and Bucky Hart. The next Scott was lying stunned on the floor, his mouth full of blood.

"Turner, you clown!" Lewis hollered. "Don't you know better'n to aim at the head?"

"Can I help it if he's short?" Art asked, laughing as he gazed at Scott's groggy body.

As for Scott, he only half heard what followed. His eyes detected only a blur of light, and he groped for something to hold on to.

"Stay where you are," Dale said, kneeling beside him. "You got busted good."

Three or four teammates helped Scott to the locker room, and Dale got a wet rag and cleaned up his face.

"Maybe I ought to call your uncle," Dale said. "You look like a mess."

"He knows," Scott said, feeling Tiaf's soft voice echo through his ears.

"He can't, Scott," Dale explained. "Man, you're out of your head, aren't you?"

"My head? No, not out of . . . I'm . . ."

"Better lie on a bench, Scott," Dale advised. "Lew's bringing some ice."

"Sure," Scott said, easing his shoulders back. Lewis French appeared presently with an ice bag, and Scott held it against his mouth. His nose was swollen, and his lip continued to bleed.

"I'll get that Turner," Lewis promised. "You wait and see, Scott. Cheap shot creep!"

"It's okay," Scott said as the cobwebs began to clear from his eyes. "I'm all right."

"Sure, you're all right," Dale grumbled. "At least all your teeth are still there. You're going to look awful blue tomorrow, though. Gee, it's a shame you didn't do this at Halloween. We could've used you at the Haunted House."

Scott tried to laugh, but his teeth ached, and his head throbbed. It wasn't the usual kind of ache, the deep pounding that usually followed a vision. This was a dull pain that started at his nose and seemed to spread all the way down his chin.

"Help me sit up," Scott said, regaining his senses. "I'd better clean myself up. The period's probably about over."

"Help him get a shower," Lewis told Dale. "Me, I want to have a talk with Turner."

"That'll be a fair match," Dale said as he helped

Scott out of his bloody shirt. "Wish I could see it. Mrs. Hunt's sure to make a good referee."

Scott tried to grin, but his mouth was too swollen. Instead he shed his clothes and let Dale lead him to the shower. A cool spray washed away the worst of the blood and eased the pain. But it wasn't the bruised and swollen face that concerned Scott.

Where did the clouds go? he wondered. He'd never lost a vision like that before. He'd been given a warning, and now it had vanished.

That had never happened, and it scared him.

8

Scott said nothing that afternoon when Lauren's mother drove him to the tall house on Cottonwood Road. His face remained swollen and bruised, and his head buzzed.

"Maybe I ought to help you to the door," Lauren offered. "If your uncle's not home, I could stay awhile."

"He'll be home," Scott assured her.

"I guess he will be," Mrs. Logan commented. "This strange uncle of yours never seems to go out at all, Scott."

"He pretty much keeps to himself," Scott explained. "Bye. Thanks for the ride, Mrs. Logan."

"Scott?" Lauren called as he stepped out the cargo door and hurried toward the house. He merely gave her a backhanded wave and continued on.

Tiaf was waiting in the front hall.

"I know," Scott said as he dumped his books on a chair. "I got distracted."

Tiaf nodded, then examined the distorted flesh, especially Scott's puffy lip and battered nose.

"You could have mended this yourself," Tiaf complained as he erased the bruises and mended the tear in Scott's lip. "Better?"

"Too much so," Scott answered. "They'll be suspicious if it heals too fast."

Tiaf scowled as Scott reproduced the outward signs of injury. Scott saw no point to including the pain, though.

"The life of an Earther is not altogether an easy one," Tiaf observed.

"No," Scott agreed. "It's strange, though. Up to today I've felt like an outsider, somebody out of place who didn't belong. You should've seen the other guys when I got hurt. They were actually worried! A busted lip and a bruised nose are almost worth it."

"I did see," Tiaf said. "I also heard your friend's mother. She's growing suspicious."

"Maybe you should meet her."

"You forget, Scott. You were born on this world. You know what's expected."

"You've been here ages, I thought."

"There's a difference. I have never been one of them."

"You think we should leave, don't you? You're worried somebody will find out. How? I've been careful."

"And fortunate. In a hospital, under anesthetic, what might you have said?"

Scott frowned and made his way to a small table. He sat down and dropped his head into his hands.

"There's something else, Tiaf," Scott said nervously. "I saw something . . . a storm. Lightning flashed out, headed straight for me. Then the ball hit."

"Yes?"

"I can't regain the vision. It's gone. It was a warning, wasn't it?"

"Possibly."

"And I can't find it again. What if I've lost my sight?"

"You can lose an arm, a leg, even a nose," Tiaf said, trying to raise Scott's spirits with a grin. "A seer can't lose the power. It is with him always."

"You're certain?"

"It's nothing to concern yourself with. The vision will come again."

"You're worried about what I'll do?"

"Yes, Scott. And something else. It is possible to turn your mind away from the vision. Can it be you don't wish to view the image?"

Scott shivered at the thought. It was all too possible. Maybe deep down he was fighting off the warning, hoping to avoid another Wichita.

The notion was never far from his mind those next few days. It was true that he was finding a new belonging at Clearmont. More and more his classmates shared jokes or greeted him with smiles. He even managed an uneasy truce of sorts with Art Turner. The lunch table he shared with Lauren and Dale added a new face daily, and while helping Lewis French select a book from the library or tutoring eighth-grade math students after school, he took note of a growing satisfaction swelling inside him.

He joined in the singing down at the Dairy Queen, and he actually sank a shot or two during a P.E. basketball game. Best of all, Lauren's family sort of adopted him, and riding home in the van after school or tossing baseballs with Dale helped fill the emptiness left by the loss of Sharon and his family.

It meant, of course, neglecting Tiaf and the lessons which expanded his talents. The old man seemed to sense Scott's need for something else just then, though.

"We'll resume when you're ready," Tiaf explained.

And what of the vision? Scott wondered.

"It, too, will come," Tiaf's voice whispered through Scott's mind.

But as the days passed, Scott found his thoughts filled only with schoolwork and the idle business of being fourteen. He helped Miss Ponds set up her telescope one night and then amazed a dozen curious classmates by locating the moons of Jupiter. The next day being Thursday, he accompanied Lauren to the baseball field to watch Dale's Falcons tangle with the rival Tigers.

"It's not too late to join the team, you know," Dale said as he played catch with Scott prior to the game. "We've got two extra uniforms."

"No, I think everyone's better off with me in the stands," Scott explained.

"Besides," Bucky Hart chipped in, "he likes Lauren."

"Yeah?" she called from the bleachers. "What's not to like?"

Bucky made his escape to the bat rack, and Scott left Dale to join his teammates. As the players gave a shout and took the field, Scott slipped past Lauren's parents and younger brothers to where she sat holding out a bag of peanuts. She cracked one open and handed him a nut. He gobbled the peanut, then took a handful from the bag.

"Your lip's about healed," she observed, touching the faint crack that remained.

"So I guess there'll be no more sympathy, huh?"

"Never was any," she said, laughing. "Sympathy? You'll get none from me so long as your geometry average stays at 98!"

"Want me to mess up some to make you feel better?"

"That would make the whole class breathe easier."

"First thing tomorrow I stop doing homework."

She laughed, then cracked a peanut. For fifteen minutes they observed the game. It was typical Zoo League, mostly strikeouts and ground balls. When Dale came up to bat, he tipped his hat and lined the ball softly to the first baseman.

"What a ham!" Lauren grumbled. "Hey, Logan, you're supposed to hit the ball!" she shouted.

"Love you, too, Sis!" Dale replied.

That was when Scott first noticed the clouds. They were mere wisps of white fluff in the beginning. But by the third inning, their undersides grew black and foreboding. There was no thunder, no hint of lightning. But Scott heard the first and saw the second.

He closed his eyes, and a flash tore the heavens. Bright yellow flame cut across the diamond. Players seemed to explode. Shirts and shoes were blasted from chests and feet. At second base Dale stared in wonder as the ground beneath him erupted. He jumped and then settled earthward again. His scorched hands and ankles twitched a second before growing still. His soft blue eyes stared wildly, silently skyward.

Scott blinked away the horrible image. His shoulders shook violently, and Lauren tried to calm him.

"What's wrong?" she asked as he gazed at the darkening sky.

"Nothing," he said, gripping the bench with both hands.

"Something sure is."

"Oh, I've had a touch of something all week."

"Ever since that dodgeball knocked you senseless," she observed. "Want me to get Mom and Dad to drive you home?"

"No," he told her.

"I can walk you."

"No, I'll be okay," he assured her. "I just need to get a drink of water."

"I'll go with you," she offered.

"No, stay and watch the game. Dale will be up soon."

Lauren reluctantly agreed. Scott hopped down from the bleachers and headed for the water fountain. His

80

eyes searched the field. How could he stop a blast of lightning? Deflecting boulders was one thing, but . . .

The vision returned. The scoreboard read 2–1, and there were two outs. Dale crouched a few feet from second base, chomping a mouthful of gum and waiting for Chip Turner to hit the ball.

What can I do? Scott asked himself.

Then he noticed an electrical switching box on a light pole behind the concession stand. There was a single knob there controlling the flow of electricity to the four banks of floodlights. It was a simple matter to cut the power. To prevent anyone from doing this, the park department detailed a man to watch the spot.

"It's the only way," a voice whispered inside Scott's head.

I know, he answered.

Telekinesis was still a fairly new skill for Scott. He had no choice but to try it, though. He shut his eyes and concentrated on the switch. His mind erased each distracting sound and sight until only the switch remained. Then, concentrating with all his might, Scott directed the knob to move.

It should have been easy. Tiaf would have done it in an instant. Scott lacked practice, though, or perhaps the blow to his chin had somehow altered his abilities. He blinked away a tear and gazed back at the field. The Falcons had gone down in order, and the Tigers already had one man out. The next boy lifted a pop-up to right field. Chip Turner now stepped to the plate. The cloud overhead seemed to rumble a warning.

No! Scott cried inside. In an instant his mind cleared, and he focused on the knob. It glowed red, then white. Finally it turned, and the field was bathed in darkness.

"What's happening?" someone cried.

A small child whined, and another screamed.

"That's it, folks!" the umpire called, waving a flashlight toward the concession stand. "Boys, let's clear the field! Blackout!"

The players grumbled and trudged from the field. Chip Turner tossed his bat at the backstop. Then the sky overhead exploded, and the fiery bolt cut across the empty infield. Players and spectators alike were flung to the earth, and screams tore through the night. Once the clamor died down, someone reached up and turned the switch. The lights flashed back on, and the crowd stared in wonder at the black scar of upturned earth etched across the baseball diamond.

"Lord, look at that!" the umpire called.

"I was just out there!" Chip Turner added.

"Look at second base," Bucky Hart shouted.

A gentle rain began to sprinkle down from overhead, and the umpire waved his arms wildly.

"That's all for tonight, folks!" the man declared. "Can't play ball in the rain."

Startled parents collected their children and headed for waiting cars. Coaches shook their heads in dismay. The park department employee stared at the switch.

"How in the world . . . ?" he muttered.

A shaken Dale Logan clung to his father's side. Lauren raced over and gripped Scott's arm.

"You had a premonition of some kind," she whispered. "You knew that was going to happen."

Scott felt a familiar fear grip his insides. He trembled.

"I saw the whole thing," her brother Drew said, joining them. "It was like magic. He looked at the light pole, and the lights went off."

"He did not," Lauren said, shaking her head. "That's impossible."

"I know," Drew agreed. "But I watched him, and—"

"Must have been a power outage," Lauren objected. "Maybe somebody in the concession stand overloaded a circuit."

"Maybe," Drew said, clearly unconvinced. "That what it was, Scott?"

"What else?" he asked. "Lights don't turn themselves off."

"No," Drew admitted. He then turned and plodded along to where Donny stood holding open the cargo door of the van.

"Lauren? Scott?" Mrs. Logan called, holding up a thin sheet of clear plastic. "Come on out of the rain, you two!"

"I'm going to hang around here a few minutes," Scott answered. "Thanks, though."

"I'm staying, too," Lauren added.

"It's raining," Mr. Logan objected. "You'll both catch cold."

"We'll be fine, Dad," Lauren assured her father. "It's just a cloudburst."

"Well, if it doesn't stop soon, we'll head home," he said. "We can drop Scott off on the way."

"Okay!" she agreed, turning Scott toward the concession stand.

9

They huddled together beneath a narrow overhang on the back side of the stand. A few feet away two park department employees inspected the switch. A crowd of curious onlookers mumbled about fate and coincidence while the players sipped Cokes and cracked jokes.

Scott said nothing, just massaged away a pain throbbing through his forehead. Rain pelted the overhang, creating a kind of musical hammering.

"I've always wondered about psychics," Lauren told him. "How did it happen?"

"What?" Scott asked as the pounding abated.

"The premonition. Was it just a flash inside your head? What did you see?"

"You don't want to know," he warned.

"I do," she insisted. "Did you see the lightning, the blackout, what?"

He got to his feet and trotted over to a deserted park pavilion. Lauren pursued him.

"I have to know," she insisted.

"I saw Dale," he explained, trembling.

Lauren's face grew pale, and she leaned her head on Scott's shoulder.

"It must have been terrible," she told him. "To see something about to happen, knowing there's nothing you can do about it."

"Yes," Scott agreed. It's not a lot better intervening, either, he thought.

"Did it just come to you? Did you get glimpses? What?"

"You don't understand, do you?" he asked. "I don't want to talk about it. It's important nobody know. You can't tell anybody, Lauren. Promise me that?"

"Why?" she asked.

"Because they won't understand. They'll call me names, make jokes. And I'll have to leave."

"Why?"

"They'll ask questions."

"So? I watch fortune-tellers on television all the time. Is it so different than reading a horoscope?"

"Very different," he muttered. Yes, he thought. Different was the word for it . . . for him.

"It's a gift, Scott," she whispered. "You shouldn't be ashamed to have people know. I'd brag about it myself."

"No, you wouldn't," he objected. "You don't know."

"Know what?"

"How it starts. Your friends begin to wonder about you. Your family grows concerned. Then strange people

86

you never saw before follow you around, snooping into your past, searching for any little detail they can use to hurt you. They can't stand not knowing, Lauren. They never give you a minute's peace. They'll poke my bones, take X rays, bring in all sorts of experts to figure things out."

"This isn't the first time, is it?" she asked.

"No," he admitted. "The last time I ended up losing my family! You can't imagine what that's like! It's been so long since I've even had friends. Now, well, it could happen all over again."

"We'll stick by you, Scott," Lauren promised.

"Then prove it by swearing you won't say anything. Make Drew promise, too."

"Drew won't say anything," she assured him. "He has strange dreams. He used to talk about them until people started making fun of him. Now he keeps everything inside. It's why he's so quiet, I guess."

"Is that why you wanted to know?" Scott asked.

"No, there was another reason."

"Oh?"

"Scott, I used to have this friend," she began, swallowing hard and turning away while she rubbed her eyes. "George Kincaid."

"The boy who died?" Scott asked.

"You know?"

"Dale told me," Scott explained. "Go on."

"George had dreams, too. He had this terrible fear of heights. I thought it was, you know, just a phobia. I don't like high places much myself. But George told me he had dreams of falling, tumbling through a terrible dark space. One day when we were twelve he told me, 'Lauren, one of these days I'm going to fall a long ways. And when I land, I'll be dead.' "

"Did he?"

"Yes," she said, gripping Scott's hand tightly. "Just that way, too. We were down by the creek, a whole bunch of us. George wandered off up a hill. Suddenly we heard this terrible scream. He fell down a well shaft. We couldn't see or hear him, and all I could think of was that George was down in that cold dark place, maybe hurt bad, and there was nothing we could do. When the fire department found him, he was dead. His neck was broken. He knew it was going to happen, didn't he?"

"Maybe," Scott remarked. "But it might just have been a dream. An accident like that . . . Well, if he'd really seen it beforehand, he could have avoided it."

"Is that how it is for you? You just run away when you see lightning's going to strike? You could warn somebody, you know. You weren't the one who was going to be hurt."

"Sometimes, most times, warning doesn't work," he told her. "People look at you as if you're crazy. They stare, and laugh, and the warning goes unheeded."

"So what do you do?" she asked.

"What I can," he told her. "Now, no more questions. You have to trust that I know best this time."

She nodded, and they headed back to the concession stand. As they sat beneath the overhang, Dale, Bucky Hart, and another eighth grader, Billy Jarvis, joined them. The three soggy players seemed to be enjoying the excitement more than they had the game.

"Did you see that lightning, Scott?" Dale asked.

"Man, if those lights hadn't gone out, we'd've been popcorn," Billy added.

"I had my shoes knocked off!" Bucky declared, showing the reddish rings around his ankles.

"I read once about a kid who had all his clothes blown off by lightning," Dale said, laughing loudly. "That sure would have made a picture for the paper, huh?"

"Been better if it'd been the girls' team," Billy added.

The three younger boys laughed and joked and rolled around like three clowns. Scott slid along the wall of the stand and did his best to escape. Lauren grasped his arm and held him in place.

"Hey, Scott, don't you want to see Bucky's ankles?" Dale asked.

"I've seen ankles before," Scott declared.

"Not like these," Bucky claimed. "The hairs on my legs are all singed."

Scott finally broke away and trotted to the curb. Just then Mr. Logan drove the van over, and little Donny slid the cargo door open.

"Game's over!" Lauren's father shouted. "Time to head home, gang."

Dale waved farewell to his friends and sprinted to the open door.

"Can we drop Scott?" Lauren called.

"Sure," her father answered. "Come on, kids."

"I can get home on my own," Scott replied. "I feel like walking."

"I'm going with him," Lauren declared.

"It's raining, kids," Mr. Logan protested. "You'll catch cold. Your clothes are already soaked, and the wind's coming down from the north. Get in the van. Walk another time."

Lauren gazed at Scott with pleading eyes, and he reluctantly trudged along to the vehicle. They got in together, and Donny slid the door shut. Mr. Logan put the van in gear, and it roared off down the street.

Scott kept silent as the van covered the three-quarters of a mile to Cottonwood Road. Dale did most of the talking, mixing in comments about the game with the close call at second base. When Mr. Logan stopped in front of the tall house at the edge of the wheatfield, Scott slid open the door and stepped out.

"I had a good time," he told the Logans. "Thanks."

"Want me to come in with you awhile?" Lauren whispered.

"It's pretty late," Scott told her. "My uncle's probably waiting for me. You better go on home. I'll see you tomorrow."

"Sure," she said, waving good-bye as Donny slid the cargo door shut. She continued waving as the van made a U-turn and rolled back down Cottonwood Road. Scott splashed his way to the door. It opened, and Tiaf's anxious eyes greeted him.

"So, it came again, as I said it would," Tiaf whispered.

"Yes," Scott muttered.

"Come along. Let's get you dried."

"Angry?" Scott asked.

"Concerned," Tiaf explained.

Scott smiled as he shed his wet clothes. Tiaf produced two warm, fluffy towels, and Scott rubbed the moisture out of his bones while Tiaf worked on Scott's hair.

Afterward, Scott stretched out on a sofa, and Tiaf ran the sonic vibrator across the boy's back. The steady hum worked a general weariness from Scott's joints and eased his anxieties. Half an hour afterward, Tiaf prepared an herbal tea, and Scott sipped a cup while the old man studied the evening's events as they flashed across a small viewing screen.

"You were noticed," Tiaf observed, pointing to Drew Logan. The boy looked on as the switch seemingly moved on its own. "He suspects you did it."

"How could he?" Scott asked. "Besides, he's Lauren's brother. He won't say anything."

"Perhaps," Tiaf said, unconvinced. "Perhaps not."

"I had to do it," Scott said. "It's just like with the sign. They would never believe I knew the lightning would hit. Then when it did, they would've called me a freak."

"You know the dangers, Scott."

"Dale's my friend, Tiaf. I had no choice."

"Each time you act this way, you alter the flow of time. You change events from their natural course."

"So history is changed. It might be for the better, you know."

"For better or worse, it has been altered."

"And who's to say that when you contacted me you weren't changing destiny? Nobody can know these things for certain."

"We can know," Tiaf objected. "The future is easily read."

Tiaf pointed to the screen, but Scott refused to look. For once the present seemed to offer a hint of belonging and peace. He didn't wish it spoiled by tomorrow.

"We should resume your lessons," Tiaf finally whispered.

"More boulders?" Scott asked.

"New challenges," Tiaf told him. "Tomorrow you will have school. Saturday we will study."

"Sure," Scott agreed. "And now I'd better get some sleep."

He placed his teacup on the table and headed back to the sleeping compartments. As he exchanged the towel for pajamas, he listened as Tiaf tinkered with the ship's machinery.

He's prepared for another journey, Scott thought. He hoped it was only a part of Saturday's lesson. He feared different.

When Scott closed his eyes, his mind floated through a dream full of wanderings. He and Tiaf walked beside the pyramids in Egypt, journeyed up the Nile, viewed the great Victoria Falls. Later they explored the realm of elephants and lions, sang with natives in a village that seemingly knew no time.

From such a pleasant scene flowed a far more cruel reality. Scott again found himself sitting in the bleachers, chomping peanuts and cheering on the Falcons. The cloud then reappeared, and he gazed on, trembling, as lightning crashed earthward. Again Dale's burned and broken body lay lifeless before him, and Scott awoke, shaking, in a cold sweat.

A new scene then flooded his brain. Scott sat bare-chested on a doctor's examination table inside a sanitized research hospital. His head was shaved, and electrode wires were attached to his temples. All around him men in white coats looked on as a colleague poked fingers in Scott's stomach, examined his nose and ears.

"His fingers appear normal," the examiner spoke into a tape recorder. "Wrists and forearms exhibit development within the norms for a boy of fourteen."

Suddenly the doctor grinned broadly.

"Gentlemen, there appear to be marked differences in the lenses of his eyes. Make a note to dissect the eyeballs of the other one when you perform the autopsy."

"Other one?" Scott gasped, tearing the electrodes from his head and rushing toward the door. Two muscular giants blocked his escape. Even so, Scott was able to view a cart in the hall. A white sheet was draped over a body.

Scott shook off the nightmare and tumbled out of the narrow slab of a bed and onto the floor. He rose slowly, ignoring the pain from a twisted ankle as he tried to erase the vision.

"Scott?" Tiaf called.

"You saw?" Scott asked. "Oh, Tiaf, it wasn't you?"

"Not me," Tiaf said as Scott rushed to his side. The

thought of being alone, the terror that now there would be no one else, no one to teach and guide and, most of all, understand, sent a wave of panic through Scott.

"You warned of the danger," Scott said, fighting to regain his composure. "I never dreamed of . . ."

"Now you have," Tiaf said, ushering Scott back to the bed. "But you have not viewed the future, not this time. All you saw happened in the past."

"What?"

"Did you imagine you and I were the only Antrians? Didn't you ever consider others had come here, too?"

"There was another boy?"

"Two," Tiaf explained. "Not so unlike yourself. I could not reach them, Scott. And so they were destroyed."

"By whom?" Scott asked.

"Some would say by their own rashness."

"It's what you fear I'll do, too."

"Yes," Tiaf confessed. "And why I urge caution."

10

At school Friday it seemed nobody could talk of anything other than the mysterious light failure at the baseball field and the subsequent lightning bolt that had rocked the infield.

"Had yourselves a close call, eh, Dale?" Brad Parker joked as the students waited outside for the early bell to ring.

"They sure did," Lewis French added. "For a while we thought they'd have to change their names from Fulton Falcons to Fulton French Fries."

Scott did his best to chase the memory of his vision from his mind. Dale seemed to enjoy all the attention, though.

"Truth is, it was pretty scary," Dale confessed. "I mean when you think about it, if I'd been out there a few minutes later, when that lightning hit, I'd've been a French fry all right—a crispy one. You know they call third base the hot corner, but second was just about charcoal city!"

The others laughed, and Dale went on with his stories. When Bucky Hart arrived, he showed off the singed hairs on his legs and the faint red rings around his ankles.

"Pretty weird how those lights went out," Lewis observed.

"My mom says it was a miracle," Bucky boasted.

"No, it was the electric company," Dale said, grinning.

The bell rang before the discussion got completely out of hand. And though the school echoed with all manner of exaggerated tales, Scott was able to avoid most of it himself. He concentrated instead on English and math and history. By the late afternoon, though, his mind began to drift. As Miss Ponds evaluated the week's lab reports, Scott found himself a world away, walking among the lions of Africa.

If he'd been less distracted, he clearly would have noticed the small can of sewing machine oil Art Turner drew from his pocket. Scott should have seen how Art dripped a bit more oil on the floor each time Miss Ponds scribbled a score on the front board until a fair-sized slick occupied the center aisle of the lab.

"Scott, your work fell off some this week," the teacher said as she posted the final two marks on the board.

"I'll try to be better," Scott promised, snapping out of his trance.

"I'm sure you will," Miss Ponds remarked. "Why

don't you come up and pass back the lab manuals. Look over your work, students, and let me know if you have any questions."

The class nodded, and Scott started up the aisle toward the small table where the manuals were stacked. On the third step Scott's left foot struck oil, and he did an instant half flip. Only a swift move of his right hand kept Scott's head from slamming against the floor. Even so, his shoulder and back crashed against the hard vinyl tiles, and he heard his wrist snap.

"Scott?" Miss Ponds called.

Art Turner laughed heartily, but the rest of the class remained silent. Scott clutched his wrist and fought the urge to scream.

"Lewis, can you help Scott to the clinic?" Miss Ponds asked.

Lewis French cautiously avoided the spilled oil. He then assisted Scott to his feet.

"You okay?" Lewis asked.

Scott gritted his teeth and nodded. Miss Ponds handed them a clinic pass, then turned angrily to deal with Arthur Turner.

"Shame to miss this," Lewis said as the teacher started in on Art. "I'll bet he catches it good. You ought to have your uncle sue him. I'll bet you have to go to the hospital. That wrist looks broken for sure."

"It'll be all right," Scott replied.

"Look at it, Scott," Lewis argued. "It's bent crazy, and swollen, too. Broken for sure. You aren't walking too good, either. Did you hit your head?"

"Shoulder," Scott explained.

"Hurts?"

"Like blazes," Scott admitted. "Once the shock wears off, it won't be too bad, though."

"Jerry Rodney cracked his clavicle, his collarbone, that way. Better get an X ray."

Scott shuddered at the mention of X rays. And when they reached the clinic, the nurse wanted to call an ambulance.

"No, I'll be fine once I get home," Scott insisted.

"Can I call your mom, Scott?" the nurse asked as she applied an ice pack.

Suddenly Scott's eyes grew moist. He recalled how his mother had rushed to the school when he'd sprained an ankle back in third grade. He could still feel her soft, delicate hands, could hear the gentle, sympathetic whisper of her voice.

"Scott?" the nurse asked, slipping his arm into a sling.

"I don't live with my mom," he explained. "My uncle doesn't have a phone."

"Oh, that's right," the woman said. "You're the nephew of that old hermit on Cottonwood Road."

"He's not a hermit."

"Well, he hasn't been seen by a soul," the nurse said, shaking her head. "Anyway, you ought to see a doctor straight off. School's about over. I'd be happy to drive you to the hospital."

"A friend's mom will be waiting for me," Scott explained. "Thanks, but I'll be fine."

The nurse seemed unconvinced, but Scott steadfastly

refused to reconsider. When the dismissal bell rang, he made his escape out the office door, then hurried through the hall to the front door of the school. He hoped to avoid Lauren, but his legs ached, and he wasn't able to get outside before she cut him off.

"I hope that Art Turner gets shipped off to reform school," Lauren griped. "He's always pulling something like this!"

Scott stopped a minute. Closing his eyes, he saw a sheepish Art Turner pleading for mercy with Mr. Howland, the principal. It almost raised a smile on Scott's lips.

"Don't worry about him," Scott said as he moved past her and headed out past the parking lot.

"Where do you think you're going?" she called. "Scott, you look like you're dying! Mom'll have the van here in a minute. We'll take you over to the hospital."

Scott sighed. He thought he'd been through that already in the clinic.

"Lauren, if you really want to help, see if Dale will run in and get my books. I forgot all about them."

"They're in your locker," she explained. "Leave them there for once. You can't very well write with an arm in a sling."

"All right," Scott grumbled. "But I still don't . . ."

"Look, Mom'll get you home, okay? Talk to your uncle. I'll come over in about an hour. If you need a ride to the hospital or to some doctor, we'll take you."

"I don't need a doctor, Lauren. I just want to get home. I appreciate your offer, but really . . ."

"There's Mom now," Lauren declared, pointing to the van rolling to the curb. "Come on. No more arguing."

Scott turned to follow her to the van. Donny and Drew raced along ahead of him, and Dale came along behind.

"Scott?" Mrs. Logan asked, frowning as he eased his way into the back seat.

"He got nailed by Art Turner," Dale explained. "It's all over school. Turner squirted oil on the floor, and Scott tripped and broke his arm."

"It's not broken," Scott complained.

"Really?" Lauren asked, touching his wrist lightly. Scott's face revealed the pain flashing up his arm, and she frowned.

"It'll be all right," Scott insisted. "Once the soreness works itself out, and the swelling goes down, I'll be as good as new."

"We'll see," she said. "One hour, Scott."

Mrs. Logan pulled the van to a stop, and Donny slid the door open. Scott stepped out, waved good-bye with his good left hand, then headed for the front door.

Once inside, Scott gazed out the front window. Lauren's mother was in no hurry to leave. He closed his eyes, cleared his mind, and envisioned the scene in the van.

"We should take that boy to the emergency room," Mrs. Logan argued. "I saw his face when you touched that arm. Lauren, I'm going right up there and tell that tightfisted uncle to take care of it."

"Mom, don't," Lauren pleaded.

"He's so thin you'd think he hadn't eaten in a year. Maybe he hasn't. Nobody ever sees Mr. Stone at a market. I'm not sure the old man even exists."

"I'll come back over in an hour," Lauren promised. "I told Scott I'd wait that long. His arm isn't going to fall off, Mom."

"Maybe not," Mrs. Logan admitted. "But I'm coming along to see for myself. And if that arm looks as bad as I suspect, I'm taking Scott to see a doctor if I have to call the sheriff's office for assistance!"

Scott didn't know whether to laugh or cry. It warmed him to know people were so concerned about his well-being. He knew, though, that a nosy Mrs. Logan would only bring new trouble and more problems. The sheriff! That's all he needed.

"Your friends grow suspicious," Tiaf observed as he joined Scott in the front room.

"They're good people. I should have said I lived with my great-aunt Mathilda. We could have projected a little old lady who could go to market and hang up washing."

"Perhaps it would have been better," Tiaf said, smiling at the notion. "Now, what have you done to yourself this time?"

"Slipped in some oil," Scott explained.

Tiaf placed a hand to Scott's head and read his memory.

"You didn't see it?" Tiaf asked.

"I was preoccupied with last night."

"That's dangerous. What if you had been sent to the hospital?"

"I could always escape."

"And not reveal yourself? I don't like this."

"I'm none too thrilled myself. Come on, Tiaf. Help me get out of this sling. I can mend the bones, can't I?"

"We'll see, won't we?"

Tiaf helped remove the sling, and he also set aside the ice pack. The wrist was misshapen, and Tiaf helped Scott straighten it.

"Concentrate on the bones," Tiaf urged. "The larger is fractured. It pains you?"

"Considerably," Scott confessed. He then swept everything from his mind and focused on the bones. He suddenly found himself seeing something akin to a large X ray, the two bones in such detail that Scott saw the break in the radius. He then formed a new image in place of the fracture, and the pain began to subside. Bit by bit the break faded until only the new radius replaced the old.

"Good," Tiaf proclaimed as Scott relaxed. "There is no trace of fracture. You have the healing touch."

Scott only half believed the change. The pain, the swelling, the discomfort . . . they were all gone.

"Now, your shoulder," Tiaf said, running the sonic vibrator along the bruised and battered muscles.

Scott concentrated again. He found no damaged bones, not even the damaged clavicle Lewis had suspected.

"You would never have been able to walk about with a broken collarbone," Tiaf argued. "As for the muscles, the vibrator will ease their soreness."

"Thank you, Tiaf," Scott said, sighing as the last of the pain left his weary body.

"Not all trouble is so easily put right, though."

"No," Scott agreed. "You mean Mrs. Logan."

"It's not only her suspicions, Scott. There are others. I've noticed more company of late. Idle visitors lurk around the house. A sheriff's car visited yesterday."

"You didn't say anything."

"I didn't wish to spoil your evening. Still, I hear and see many thoughts in this town. We have no close neighbors, but I witness many callers."

"Do you talk with them?"

"No," Tiaf explained. "It's better we remain a mystery than for anyone to identify our origin or direction."

"You think we should leave, don't you?"

"Yes," Tiaf said, sitting beside Scott and looking deeply into his eyes. "There is so much danger."

"And yet you've stayed."

"It pains me to see you unhappy, lonely."

"Will it always be this way?" Scott asked, shuddering at the idea.

"You are the seer, my young friend. What does your mind tell you?"

"It's not my mind that's asking, Tiaf. It's my heart."

"Even so, look and tell me what you see."

Scott placed his fingers to his forehead and searched

for some hint of what lay ahead. Nothing appeared. His mind remained as empty as a bottomless well.

There was a knock at the door then, and Tiaf stepped aside.

"Your friend," he announced.

Scott nodded, then made his way to the door. He found Lauren and her mother side by side.

"Ready?" Mrs. Logan asked.

"For what?" Scott asked.

"To go to the hospital," Lauren said, folding her arms angrily against her chest. "Your wrist . . ."

"Is fine now," Scott said, opening the door and stepping outside. "See. All it needed was some ice and a little salve."

"Well, would you look at that!" Mrs. Logan cried. "It's as if . . . Tell your uncle I'd like to try some of his salve on my feet, Scott. I never saw such a thing in all my life!"

"Mom, you can go on home, I guess," Lauren said, escorting her mother toward the waiting van. "I'll be along later. I want to talk to Scott."

"All right, dear," Mrs. Logan agreed. Moments later the van made its wide swing around the road and headed back as it had come. Lauren led Scott to the shade of a nearby apple tree and sat down underneath.

Scott joined her. They said nothing, just gazed out past the field at the distant horizon.

"You all right?" Lauren finally whispered.

"You seem to spend an awful lot of your time asking me that these days," Scott told her.

"I guess that's because you seem to be so lost, Scott."

"I am lost in a way," he said sadly.

"Oh?"

"Well, misplaced at least."

"You mean because your family's gone?" Lauren asked.

"Not that so much," he explained. "It's just that I once had such a clear idea of where I was going, who I was, and what I'd be doing later on. Now it's all a muddle. I feel so out of place."

"You're just mad because of that stupid Art Turner."

"It's not that at all," he told her. "It's because I thought this would be a good place to start over."

"And?"

"You can't ever really start over, Lauren. Not when you're almost fifteen. Too much has happened. There are so many old dreams and memories. Then, too, you start looking around at a place and realize you're still haunted by what you did and felt before."

"But that's good. You shouldn't have to put your past away like a toy you've outgrown or a worn-out pair of shoes."

"It would be better if I could," he said, staring at his toes. "As it is, I guess I'll be leaving soon."

"I knew it!" she shouted. "It's that mean old skinflint uncle! Let me talk to him, Scott. If he doesn't want you, you can move into our house."

"You don't understand," Scott said, holding her back as she tried to rise.

"Then help me," she pleaded.

"I can't, Lauren, because I only halfway comprehend it all myself."

"When will you go?"

"Soon," he said, sighing. "A week, maybe later."

"Good. That gives me time to work on you. You'll see. This is a good place, and you can belong here as much as anywhere else. What are you doing tomorrow?"

"It's Saturday," he grumbled. "I usually have lessons with my uncle."

"Lessons?"

"Another mystery, I'm afraid."

"Well, ditch the lessons this week. We're having a party for Donny. He has his eighth birthday tomorrow. There'll be twenty or thirty kids running around Independence Park, and I'll need some help."

"Doesn't sound like much fun."

"It will be. Oh, they'll get on your nerves some, but the little ones really are funny. We'll play games, maybe clown around a little. Say you'll come."

"I don't know."

"Yes, you do. I see how you are with Dale. You enjoy helping him do his math work. You miss your brother. Here's a chance to have a whole parkful of brothers and sisters, even if it's just for one day. What do you say? You can't hide out in this gloomy old house forever!"

"Then I guess I better say yes."

"Great! We'll come by for you at nine in the morning. Don't worry about bringing anything besides yourself. We've got enough food for an army. Actually, we have an army, even if it's kind of a short one."

Her face lit up as she rose to her feet, and Scott couldn't help brightening. As she turned homeward, Scott began to wonder if perhaps he was wrong after all. Perhaps Clearmont *was* a place to make a fresh start.

11

Tiaf had been opposed to the trip to Independence Park, but Scott needed to hear laughter.

"There are preparations to make," Tiaf complained.

"I know," Scott agreed. "But it's just this once, and Lauren's so excited. You know how much I miss Brian. It's one last chance to be part of a family. Do you understand?"

"Yes," Tiaf said sadly.

And so Scott found himself wedged into Lauren's van that next morning as her mother drove to Independence Park. Restless seven- and eight-year-olds wrestled around behind him. Dale tickled little Donny while Lauren did her best to maintain order. It was a hopeless task, however.

Once at the park, the children scattered in all directions. Twenty or so of Donny's friends were already there, spinning around the merry-go-round or climbing monkey bars.

108

"Pure chaos," Scott observed as he helped Lauren unload a box of games from the van.

"Be glad we're not inside," she responded. "Come on, Scott. Weren't you ever eight?"

"Seems like a long time ago," he said, stepping to his right and kicking an errant soccer ball back to some players. "A lot's happened since then."

"You couldn't always have been serious," she declared. "Admit it."

"At eight, I was a terror," he told her. "I'd bug my folks to take me this place or that, usually to the library or the planetarium. I had so many questions. . . . You just wouldn't believe how much I read."

"Yeah? You must've been like Drew then."

Scott glanced over at Drew. The eleven-year-old sat on a picnic table reading a paperback novel.

"Guess that's why I never learned to hit a baseball," Scott noted. "I could name twenty constellations in the fourth grade."

"Well, all that knowledge won't do you a lick of good today, Scott Stone. I lost the coin flip with Dale. We have to help make kites."

"That doesn't sound so bad."

"Wait and see," Lauren warned.

Sure enough, she was right. As they handed out spools of string and kites, the assorted kite fliers scrambled to assemble their craft. Nobody bothered with directions, and in a matter of minutes, the first little girl tugged on Lauren's arm for help.

"I can't get the sticks to fit," the child complained. "Can I have another kite?"

"Sorry, Holly, but they're all gone," Lauren explained. "Get Scott here to help you fix it. He knows all about kites."

"I do?" Scott asked.

"Naturally," Lauren assured him. "Anybody who could name twenty constellations when he was ten can build a kite."

Holly gazed up with wide brown eyes, and Scott waved the girl along. They found a deserted table and began rebuilding the kite.

It gave Scott considerable satisfaction to make the kite airworthy. By the time Holly made a tail of rags, he'd fitted the sticks into their slots and securely taped the flaps in place.

"Will you help me launch it?" the girl asked.

"No, that's where all the fun is," Scott said, tying on the tail. "But I'll bet if you give it a few feet of line and run real fast straight into the wind, it'll hop up there just like an eagle."

"Think so?" Holly asked, clearly unconvinced.

"Try it," Scott suggested.

She took the kite out onto a vacant stretch of hillside and ran into the wind. The little kite wagged and wiggled a bit, then plunged to the ground. Holly stared back at Scott, hands on her hips.

"Try again!" he hollered.

She did. The third try, the kite soared into the sky. And as she watched in wonderment, the little mixture of string, paper, and sticks rose higher and higher.

"Thanks, Scott," Holly yelled. She then turned away

to see if she could swing her kite above the others, and Lauren brought Scott three new customers.

"You fix kites, huh?" a small, dark-haired boy asked.

Scott shrugged his shoulders, grinned at Lauren's laughing face, and set about fixing the kites. He did, in fact, spend the better part of the morning building kites. Around eleven Lauren rescued him.

"Free at last," he whispered as she led the way toward a picnic pavilion.

"Not free," she announced. "Reassigned."

She then pointed to several packages of franks and two charcoal grills.

"Don't tell me," he grumbled. "Weenie roast?"

"You got it. We get the dogs roasted. The kids make their own hot dogs. You might set out the mustard and relish. Mom'll have the buns stacked on the far table. Mr. Fraser has the chips and drinks in his station wagon. Help him carry 'em over, okay?"

"Sure," he said, shaking his head. "Thought this was supposed to be fun."

"For them," she said, tossing a plastic wrapper at his face. "When you finish, you can probably talk Drew into swapping jobs. He's umpiring a kickball game. He hates it."

Scott tried to pout, but Lauren's sneaky smile drew his laughter. He hurried over to help Mr. Fraser. After they'd dragged ice chests and chip boxes to the pavilion, Scott set off for the chicken-wire backstop of a softball field.

"Ready for some relief?" Scott called to a weary Drew.

"You got it!" Drew yelled, tossing Scott a whistle and racing off toward the pavilion.

"You call balls and strikes," Dale yelled from second base. "I call whether they're safe or out."

"Balls and strikes?" Scott asked, gazing at a boy bouncing a ball on what was normally the softball pitcher's mound.

"Don't you know how to play kickball?" a boy asked, tapping the sunken metal plate with his toe. "It's got to cross the plate on the ground. And if it hits me, I get a free base."

"Of course," Scott said, waving for the pitcher to begin. The pitcher rolled the ball toward the plate, and the waiting boy booted it into the air. Instantly, calm little boys and girls began screaming and racing after the ball. The second baseman trapped it, then flung it full force at the back of a girl running toward third base. The ball knocked her over, and the kids yelled with delight. Scott feared the girl would be badly hurt, but she merely got to her feet, shook off a layer of sand, and trudged back to her teammates.

Umpiring was always a thankless task, and Scott soon discovered it was as true for kickball as for any other sport. The next kicker bounced the ball off the pitcher's knee, and again players shouted and scurried in a dozen directions. The ball rolled off toward the swings, and Donny Logan headed to retrieve it. He tossed it to a redheaded player, who chased a runner down the third base line. The fleeing runner jumped to avoid the ball, then hopped onto the plate.

"I tagged him!" the redhead protested when Scott motioned the runner safe.

"You missed!" the runner insisted.

"Did not!" the team in the field shouted as one.

"Did so!" the bunch at bat challenged.

In seconds the kids were battling each other over the play, and Scott did his best to intervene. It was a mistake. Kickballers were especially deadly with their toes, and Scott soon felt his shins assaulted by a pair of eight-year-old feet.

Dale finally ended the melee by blasting his whistle.

"Game over!" he shouted. "Mom's got lunch ready."

Scott supposed hunger overpowered other feelings, for the kids stampeded toward the pavilion, leaving a breathless Scott limping for safety.

"Guess you didn't know what you were getting into, huh?" Dale asked.

"You know I didn't," Scott answered. "Lauren owes me for this."

"She's good at tricking people into doing things," Dale explained as he led Scott toward the others. "I always thought you were too smart, but then you hit your head the other day, didn't you?"

"I must have," Scott said, grinning. "Hard!"

Dale slapped Scott's back and laughed loudly. Scott felt a smile spread across his face. In spite of the bruised shin, and ears near deafened by screaming kids, he warmed at the sense of belonging that enveloped him. And as he sat with Lauren on a plastic tablecloth, the two of them eating hot dogs and tossing potato chips at each other, he knew she'd been right to egg him into coming.

Scott had an easier afternoon. Parents had passed out board games and set up horseshoe pegs. Dale and Drew oversaw a game of Frisbee football. Scott helped Lauren pack up the food and clean up the pavilion. Then they walked down to where a little creek flowed through a botanical garden. In the distance a log cabin sat atop a hill.

"The first family to live in Clearmont built that place," Lauren explained. "When they arrived, they lived in a cave back behind the cabin. Once they hid there three days while Indians camped at the creek."

"Good thing they didn't have any of Donny's friends," Scott pointed out. "Noise would've brought the Indians in a hurry."

"One look at that bunch," Lauren said, pointing to the quarreling Frisbee players, "would have sent the Kiowas fleeing for the hills."

"Maybe so," Scott admitted.

His smile faded though as a face flashed inside his head. Then another. There were two small figures in a dark hole. They laughed and raced along, shouting at someone behind them. There was a terrible rumble. Wood splintered, and the earth seemed to shudder. Screams pierced the air.

"You said there was a cave?" Scott asked, trembling as he leaned against a nearby oak.

114

"About a hundred yards ahead," she answered. "Now it's sort of a historical landmark. Why do you ask? Scott, are you all right?"

His face turned gray white, and his head began to pound. The figures reappeared, their wide, frightened eyes staring in horror as the ground shook, and a world of rock and earth collapsed on top of them. An image of the mouth of the cave took shape. Then dust and debris engulfed it so that the cave itself seemed to vanish.

"Where?" he asked, gripping her by the shoulders. "What direction?"

"Just past the cabin," she explained. "Scott?"

He didn't answer. Instead he moved past her and raced on toward the cave.

12

As Scott approached the mouth of the cave, he was suddenly jerked backward.

"Scott, what are you doing?" Lauren asked.

"Come on," he told her. "We have to stop them!"

"Stop who?"

"Don't ask stupid questions," he complained. "Hurry!"

He started inside the cave, but his attention was drawn by the echo of racing feet.

"There!" he shouted as Donny Logan and a pair of companions raced out of the cave's mouth.

"Donny!" Lauren called.

The first boy poked Donny's ribs, and Donny paused only long enough to wave at his sister. Then all three turned and chased one another back inside.

"They're only playing tag," Lauren said, laughing at Scott's fearful face. "I've been in there a million times.

116

There are all sorts of beams and supports. There's nothing to worry about."

"Don't you understand anything?" Scott asked, his eyes growing wide and wild. "Come back, boys!"

The ground began to rumble then, and a crack appeared in the rock. A boulder rolled off down the hillside.

"Donny!" Lauren screamed.

Scott felt his head explode with pain, and he tried to blink away the vision as he stumbled forward. The first of the three boys reappeared, and Scott ran toward him. The others yelled frantically from deeper within the cave.

"Help!" the first boy pleaded as beams split and a cloud of dust and rock seemed to devour him. Scott flew toward him. The boy was half buried by the time Scott arrived. Scott slipped his arms under the trapped boy's armpits and pulled him out even as the roof of the cave crashed down all around them.

"Scott!" Lauren called.

He didn't answer, just hugged the freed child and turned toward her. Dust shrouded the whole hillside, and Scott could see nothing. He closed his eyes and stumbled on, trusting his instincts to guide him. When he emerged from the roiling dust, he passed his stunned bundle to waiting arms and collapsed on the ground as a crowd gathered near the cave.

"Scott! Scott!" Lauren cried.

"I'm all right," he said, rubbing the dust from his eyes.

"He saved my life," the rescued boy declared, pointing at Scott.

"And Donny?" Lauren asked.

"He and Jeremy . . ." the boy went on, staring at the dust cloud, at the fallen rock that now blocked the cave's entrance.

"Jeremy?" a woman cried. "Which Jeremy?"

"Tidwell," the trembling youngster sobbed. "We were only playing tag. We done it before. Then the cave just . . ."

"We've got to go help them!" Lauren shouted, urging Scott back to his feet. "Donny's in there!"

"Hold on," Mr. Fraser called, tugging on Lauren's hand. "Can't you see the whole front wall's given way? Listen. It's not over."

"Jack, what do we do?" one of the mothers asked, turning toward a man dressed in the uniform of a deputy sheriff.

"Contact the county fire rescue team," the deputy declared. "Straight away. And keep everybody back. I've seen these cave-ins before. Mostly they're caused by fissures. Could be we could have some rockslides. Can't have anybody else hurt."

"But my brother's in there, Mr. Porter!" Lauren objected.

"I know," the deputy told her. "But if they're still okay, we can dig 'em out."

"And if not?" Lauren asked, turning to Scott.

"We'll still bring 'em out, honey," the deputy explained. "But it sure won't do 'em any good either way to get somebody else hurt."

118

Mr. Logan then appeared, and Lauren buried her face in her father's chest. Sobbing, she explained what had happened. Scott stepped off to the side and left the Logans to comfort each other.

Deputy Porter notified the rescue squad, then sent for some shovels. In no time a group of men began picking at the debris, digging rock and soil. But each time they cleared a few feet, the ground would stir, and more earth would rain down from the hillside overhead.

"Nothing we can do till this stabilizes," Mr. Logan observed. "Meanwhile, I guess we could get some drilling equipment, jackhammers and such. Better get the kids home. It's going to be a long afternoon."

"Yes," Deputy Porter agreed. "We could use some radios. And flashlights. Lanterns'd be even better."

People began making lists of needs, and others hurried to locate each item. Scott sat beside the creek and washed the grit from his face. As he stared at his distraught face in the water, Lauren joined him.

"You saw it coming," she whispered. "I didn't understand. It's all my fault, isn't it?"

"Nobody's fault," he mumbled. "It was just an accident."

"I stopped you. You could have gotten them out in time."

"I got one," Scott said, shaking as he gazed at the cave.

"Oh, Scott, I can't stand it. Donny could be in there, suffocating. Or he could be lying under some rock, dying. He could be dead already!"

Scott closed his eyes. His mind swept through

cracked timbers, past rock and dirt to where two half-buried boys coughed the dust from their lungs.

"Not dead," Scott declared.

He now observed legs and arms crushed by the weight of fallen beams. He felt the pain etched on those small faces. And he also saw a pair of stretchers carried to a waiting ambulance. Cold woolen blankets covered shattered bodies. Women wept, and Lauren restlessly prowled about.

"I can't just stand here helplessly," Lauren said, crying. "There's got to be something I can do."

"There's not," Scott assured her. Nor them, either, he thought, gazing back at the men who were again trying to scratch a tunnel through the mountain of debris.

"He's only eight," she whispered. "Eight today. I remember when he got his first tooth. I almost strangled him for stealing my diary last year. But, Scott, he's my brother. I love him. You know what that feels like."

"Yes," he said, sighing. "I lost my brother."

"Oh, I'm sorry," she said, gripping his shoulder with a trembling hand. "I forgot. It's just that . . ."

"I understand," he told her, rising to his feet. "Now, I want you to stop worrying. Everything will be all right."

"What?"

"Stop worrying. I'll take care of them."

"What? How?"

"I can't explain," Scott said, drawing back as she reached for his hand. "Just trust me to know."

"Scott?" she called.

But he was already gone.

13

As Scott grasped the ring and pictured in his mind the dark interior of the cave, he heard Tiaf whisper a warning.

"The danger's too great, my young friend. You dare not interfere."

But Lauren's words also haunted Scott.

"He's only eight."

In the end, warnings did no good. Caution never did. Scott could hear Donny's shallow breathing, could see the splintered bone and torn flesh. And each time he glimpsed Donny or Jeremy, Scott saw his own brother, Brian, and recalled how Brian, only ten, pulled Scott, a half-drowned twelve-year-old, from a lake when grim death was reaching out its cold, heartless arms.

"I can't tell you what to do," Tiaf told Scott. "You must decide. But if you act, we must leave."

"You knew that already," Scott said as he approached the far side of the hill. Yes, there could be a second entrance there, couldn't there? That would be his story.

He gripped the ring and concentrated with all his might. A dull hum flooded his ears. Then, in a flash of light, his molecules leaped through a fracture of space and time, wove their way through impassable rock, and reassembled in the cramped depth of the cave. There, deep within the belly of the earth, he knelt beside the two imprisoned boys.

"Donny?" Scott whispered.

Pain had overwhelmed both youngsters. Scott felt their pulses. Both were faint. Their eyes were closed, and the dust covering their faces painted a deathlike pallor.

Scott started with Jeremy. A giant beam pinned both the boy's legs. One continued to bleed while pressure had apparently clamped the arteries of the other.

"Doesn't matter," Scott declared. He focused his thoughts on the beam. Miraculously it rotted into so much sawdust. He then swept rock and dust away. Finally he stared fiercely at Jeremy's sunken chest, at shattered bones and torn arteries. Bone knitted, and flesh mended. Scott opened his eyes and observed the incredible way in which the dying child's broken body became whole once more.

"Rest now," Scott said, placing his hand on Jeremy's forehead.

Scott next turned to Donny. There were no beams or boulders crushing the eight-year-old, but Donny's left leg was bent awkwardly to one side, and four ribs were fractured. His small heart labored to pump blood, and one lung was near collapse.

Scott concentrated, but a great weariness threatened to engulf him. He coughed and dropped to one knee.

"Tiaf?" Scott called.

But Tiaf could not help. No one could.

There's only me, Scott told himself. He pressed his hands to his forehead and fixed in his mind Donny's once smiling, hopping figure. Scott's face burned, and his mind ached. He grew dizzy. A shadow of Lauren's tearstained face tried to overwhelm him. Memories of childhood, half-forgotten dreams, monsters from nightmares all tried to crowd little Donny Logan from Scott's thoughts.

No! Scott thought as he cleared all else away. Only Donny remained. Ribs did mend. The leg straightened and grew firm again.

"What's happening?" Donny whimpered as he sat up.

Scott smiled, then collapsed.

Perhaps half an hour passed before Donny was able to shake Scott to consciousness.

"How'd you get here?" Donny cried. "Where'd you come from? You were outside!"

"I came to bring you and Jeremy out," Scott said, fighting to revitalize his muscles.

"My leg," Donny mumbled. "It was—"

"It's fine," Scott declared, drawing the boy close. "You're going to be fine."

"We're trapped," Donny said, crawling over to his friend. "Jeremy? Are you dead?"

Jeremy returned to life, and the two boys cowered beside a boulder and blinked away a combination of fear and confusion.

"How'd you . . . ?"

"I came through a tunnel," Scott told them. "It's just a crack really, and it'll be a tight squeeze getting you back through it."

"It'll cave in on us!" Donny cried. "Like before."

"No," Scott said, slowly, patiently working the numbness out of his fingers. "We'll be fine."

"Can we go now?" Jeremy pleaded.

"Not just yet," Scott explained. "It was hard getting here, and I had to dig you out. I need to rest just a bit."

"But the cave could come down on us again," Donny argued.

Both boys trembled at the thought, and Scott motioned them to his side. He lightly touched their foreheads, and a gentle, peaceful sleep enveloped them.

Scott envied them that rest. He felt a hundred years' sleep wouldn't chase away the great fatigue he felt. Utter exhaustion swallowed him. But he felt the ring burning in his fist. And when his legs came back to life, he roused the boys.

"Are we going now?" Donny asked.

"Yes," Scott told them. "It's hard to explain exactly what's going to happen now. I want you to grab my arm. Hold on tight, too. We're going through the tunnel."

"What tunnel?" Jeremy asked. "I can't see anything."

"I got through, didn't I?" Scott asked. "Now stop worrying and hang on."

Scott felt their small arms clutch his sides. He gripped their hands and closed his eyes. The weariness clawed at him, but he concentrated as never before. He painted the hillside in his thoughts, smiled as the clear blue sky and the singing birds caressed his soul. Then everything began to spin. Pain surged through his entire being, and he grew dizzy.

He felt as if he were falling. Phantom hands reached out, scratched at him, fought to tear the boys from his grip. Screams slashed at his mind.

"I've seen you before, death," Scott said icily as he fought off the coldest touch of all. I've cheated you again.

And as light erupted all around him, he knew it was true. He tumbled into the soft grass of the small meadow at the base of the hillside. Glancing at the shivering boys at his elbows, Scott smiled. Then he stared up at the hillside. A crumbling passageway ate through the rock.

"We made it!" Donny said, blinking at the fading twilight.

"Look," Jeremy added, pointing at the jumble of rocks. "It's caved in. Our tunnel's gone!"

"Doesn't matter," Scott told them. "You're safe. Now, let's get you to your folks."

Donny leaned against Scott, and Jeremy wrapped a small arm around Scott's narrow waist. He was half tempted to raise the both of them onto his weary shoulders, but instead he led the way toward the far side of the hill.

Mrs. Tidwell was the first to notice the three shadowy figures stumbling toward their would-be rescuers. Exhausted men huddled nearby.

It's near night, Scott realized. Whether he'd passed out on the hillside or slept away the afternoon inside the cave, he didn't know. It mattered not at all. Jeremy raced toward his mother's waiting arms, and a great cheer rose from the collected townspeople.

Donny soon located his family and rushed toward them. Scott sought the shadow of three large willows. His fatigue prevented him from escaping entirely, but he feared an onslaught of questions and hoped to avoid the crowd.

Even so, he made no effort to evade Lauren. She trotted to him, then flung her arms around him in a grateful embrace.

"How?" she asked.

"The cave-in . . . opened up another . . . tunnel," he stammered. "I crawled . . ."

"We've been over every inch of this place," she protested. "There are no other entrances. The rescue people have been drilling oxygen vents."

"There was a tunnel," Scott repeated.

"Come on," she said, tugging him toward the others. "We've got food and cold drinks. You look exhausted. Are you hurt? Your arms look like someone's been tearing at you."

"Rocks," he explained. "Lauren, no. I'm tired. I just want to get away from here."

It was too late to escape the attention, though. Jeremy Tidwell was already leading a small army of family and friends toward Scott, and Deputy Porter wasn't far behind.

"I have to leave now," Scott told Lauren.

"Leave? No, Scott. My folks haven't even thanked you. You have to—"

He shook his head as he broke away from her grasp. He ducked under a low limb and stumbled past a rocky outcropping. Then, squeezing the ring, Scott pictured the ship, saw Tiaf's anxious face. There was a flash, and Scott vanished.

Scott rematerialized in the galley. Tiaf was waiting with warm water and towels.

"You saw?" Scott asked.

"Yes," the old man explained.

"Then you know I had no choice. I couldn't let them die."

"Perhaps not. Now we must leave, though. Already it has started."

Scott closed his eyes and envisioned a caravan of television cameras besieging the town of Clearmont. Mrs. Tidwell and Jeremy told of the miraculous escape. Others spoke of the near disaster at the baseball game.

"God watches over this town," Mrs. Tidwell declared.

"Surely someone does," Deputy Porter commented.

Scott's mind then shifted to a picture of tight-lipped Lauren Logan.

"I don't know where he went," she declared. "He's terribly shy. All this attention bothers him."

"People say you know him best of all," a reporter said. "Surely you can tell us something about him. Where did he live before coming to Clearmont? Is it true that he had a premonition about the cave-in?"

"Leave him alone!" she shouted.

"Even now they are coming," Tiaf grumbled. "I read your heart, Scott, and it is heavy. But to stay is to risk discovery, even death."

"I know," Scott admitted, glimpsing fragments of the old nightmare, images of white-frocked doctors poking and probing, taking X rays and writing reports.

"A most unusual specimen, this," one of them remarked.

"And still you acted?" Tiaf asked.

"I had to," Scott explained. "I've done a lot of thinking about this lately, Tiaf. For a long time after I left home I thought of these visions as some sort of curse. They're not. This sight of mine is a kind of gift, a special talent, and I believe I have a responsibility to use it."

Again Scott's mind clouded with images of investigators and television cameras. He gazed at Tiaf, and the old man frowned.

"I know we have to leave," Scott admitted as he washed the grime from his face. "You warned me it would happen again. It always will, I suppose."

"Probably," Tiaf said, touching Scott lightly on the shoulder.

"It's going to be awful lonely."

"As it always is."

"When do we have to go?"

"There are preparations to complete," Tiaf whispered. "Tomorrow. Now you must rest."

"Yes," Scott agreed.

After bathing and mending the scratches and tears in his skin, Scott slid wearily onto his sleeping pallet and allowed sleep to grant a brief respite from his worries.

He awoke to the sound of Tiaf rushing about the ship.

"We have company," the old man whispered through Scott's mind. "Outside, even now, they come."

Scott scrambled into his clothes and raced toward the control room. He gazed at the viewing screen. But instead of cameramen or sheriff's officers, two forlorn figures appeared in the predawn shadows.

"It's all right," Scott told Tiaf. "It's Lauren and her brother."

"And who else?" Tiaf objected. "Surely the others can't be far behind."

"I have to see them," Scott explained. "To say good-bye."

Tiaf scowled. Scott knew, too, it would be safer to leave that very moment. But he needed to hold on to some fragment of those weeks in Clearmont, so he squeezed the ring and rematerialized in the doorway of the house.

"I thought perhaps you'd already be gone," Lauren said as she greeted him.

"Not me," Dale insisted. "Friends don't run off without saying good-bye."

"Friends?" Scott asked.

"No matter what," Lauren told him. "We had to take

the phone off the hook, you know. The town's crawling with TV people. I want you to know it wasn't easy to sacrifice my shot on the morning news."

"There'll be plenty of chances yet," Scott declared.

"You mean after you're gone?" Dale asked. Scott nodded, and Dale frowned. "I figured as much. It's why your uncle never comes out. You've got this power or something."

"It's more than just knowing about things, isn't it?" Lauren asked. "Drew was right when he said you changed the switch at the ballgame, wasn't he? Deputy Porter swears that tunnel wasn't there an hour earlier, and Donny can't remember how you got him out of the cave."

"That's probably best," Scott commented.

"How'd you do it, Scott?" Dale asked. "The rescue squad says there's not so much as a crack in that hill. People can't just walk through solid rock."

"I'd say not," Scott agreed.

"How?" Lauren asked.

"You don't really want to know," he told her.

"I have to," she insisted, gripping his arm.

"All right," Scott said, taking a deep breath. "There's no great mystery to it. Nothing in the entire universe is truly solid. Everything's composed of molecular particles."

"I know all that," Lauren grumbled. "What's it got to do with the cave?"

"Everything," Scott said, trembling as he read the confusion in her eyes. He wanted to tell her, but there wasn't time. And it wouldn't help.

"Scott?" Lauren asked.

"Things aren't always what they seem," he said finally as he led Lauren and Dale away from the house, then stared sadly at the place that for a brief time had represented home. The image wavered, then melted into nothing.

"Scott?" Lauren cried again, leaning against him for support.

"Can't be!" Dale gasped.

"This will be hard to understand," he told them. "I'm not like other people. I have special talents."

"Do you ever!" Dale exclaimed.

"And now you'll go?" Lauren asked with tearful eyes. "Where?"

"Somewhere," Scott whispered. "Anywhere. Everywhere."

"I owe you so much," she said, holding on to his arm. "You saved my brother's life."

"Two of 'em," Dale added.

"It's small repayment for your gifts," Scott told them.

"Gifts?" Lauren asked.

"Your friendship," Scott explained. "Belonging. It's very rare in the world I walk."

"What?" she asked.

"Doesn't matter," Scott said, sighing. "I won't forget you."

"Me, either," Lauren promised.

"I brought my glove and a ball," Dale said, swallowing hard. "You've still got time for a game of catch, I'll bet."

Scott's mind filled with a vision of his brother Brian sadly tossing a basketball at the garage door and waiting for it to return. It would. Scott wouldn't.

He saw his mother packing a box of his old clothes away. His father stood alongside. Pain and sorrow . . . they never entirely went away.

"Scott?" Lauren called.

"It's time I went," Scott explained. He wandered off toward a distant oak tree, then gripped the ring and was gone.

"I didn't know anything else to say," Scott whispered as he stared at the viewing screen. He felt Tiaf at his side and leaned back so that the old man's hands rested on Scott's shoulders.

"You did nothing wrong," Tiaf observed.

"Then why do I feel so bad?"

"Because now we must go again. And we will be alone."

"Yes," Scott said, taking his place in the pilot's chair. Tiaf sat opposite, and the screen began to fill with images of far-off places. The Nile swept through the ancient Egyptian delta, and they sped along through time and space, watching the pageant of history pass alongside. But no matter how far they traveled, there would be no haven, no refuge.

"Must we always be wanderers, Tiaf?" Scott asked.

"It's our destiny," the old man answered sadly.

"Will it ever grow easier?"

"Was it this time?" Tiaf asked.

Scott envisioned Clearmont High that next Monday,

saw Lauren sitting alone in the cafeteria, her eyes still red from crying.

No, it wasn't easier, Scott admitted. It never would be. Messengers were, by nature, wanderers. But they were also, he supposed, adventurers and explorers. Scott thought about little Ben and his red cap, and Donny and Jeremy, reunited with their thankful parents.

Seeing was, after all, a gift. Scott had put things right, and the realization warmed him as time and space and distance flew by.

ABOUT THE AUTHOR

Author G. CLIFTON WISLER says, "Most of us have probably wished at one time or another that we could foretell the future. I think it's intriguing to see just what problems that might cause, and to examine how Scott copes with those special difficulties."

Mr. Wisler has written many award-winning books. They include *The Antrian Messenger,* an International Reading Association–Children's Book Council Children's Choice, and *Thunder on the Tennessee,* winner of the Golden Spur Award for Best Western Juvenile. He lives in Garland, Texas.

DATE DUE

Fac 12-7-92
Fac 9-6-
Fac 1/53